STORIES from SAXO
the OTHER NORSE MYTHS

Previously published translations:

The Saga of Didrik of Bern

Collections of
Scandinavian ballad translations:

Lord Peter and Little Kerstin

Warrior Lore

The Faraway North

STORIES from SAXO
the OTHER NORSE MYTHS

retold and illustrated by

IAN CUMPSTEY

Northern Displayers, Skadi Press

CUMBRIA, ENGLAND

2019

Stories from Saxo, the Other Norse Myths

Published in 2019 by Northern Displayers, Skadi Press, England
www.northerndisplayers.co.uk

ISBN 978-0-9576120-4-4

Contents

Introduction

I have chosen a series of stories from Saxo's *Gesta Danorum* and present them here, retold for a general modern reader. I have included stories that Saxo tells about the Norse gods. In some cases the gods are clear and unmistakable, but sometimes the links are more tentative. I have included stories with other mythological aspects, with magic, giants, dragons, and otherworlds. And I have included some of Saxo's heroic legends, and some legends that are related to other Norse stories known from elsewhere. Note that the stories are presented thematically, not ordered according to Saxo's timeline.

Saxo includes passages of poetry in his work, and I have occasionally rendered his verse passages also as a form of verse. At the end of the book, I have given the stories some context with notes based on the work of the authors cited in the Bibliography. I have also occasionally offered my own opinions or interpretations there, especially, but not only, as related to the Scandinavian ballads.

* * *

The *Gesta Danorum* (Deeds of the Danes) is a long work written by Saxo in Latin in Denmark around 1200. The work is made up of sixteen books. The first nine of these in particular cover more legendary material, and can give some insight into Norse myths. Much of what we read in general about Norse mythology is based on Icelandic sources; Saxo's writing is significant in that it is a major work produced outside Iceland containing material that is undoubtably related to Norse mythology (though some of Saxo's source material was Icelandic).

Things are not as straightforward as they might be, though. Saxo presents his work as a history of Danish kings, and it seems as though a range of mythological and folkloric materials were woven together and moulded to fit into this long line of kings. Sometimes it seems that Saxo reports the myths and legends faithfully. Sometimes it seems that he has made the gods human or changed their names in his versions of the myths. Sometimes it seems that he has placed contemporary human heroes into the supernatural world of the old gods and let them explore. Some of his stories have a supernatural element or a mythological aspect, and yet don't seem to correspond to anything that is known about Norse myths from other sources. Saxo is hardly unique in his approach to humanising the gods. The Icelandic writer Snorri used a similar approach in his *Prose Edda* and *Heimskringla*.

The fact that Saxo's great work is written in Latin rather than the vernacular language also makes it a little less transparent: there is no mention of the typical dwarfs or elves or others; we see supernatural creatures such as satyrs and forest maidens, and it is left to us to guess how these might have been described in the original Norse language. Even the gods are often called magicians. Names are also rendered into Latin. When this has happened by alteration of a Danish/Norse name (e.g., *Balderus*), it is sometimes clear what the original name was, though not always. But when Saxo has Latinised the names by translating them into corresponding Latin concepts (e.g., *Proserpina*, *Dis*, *Tartarus*, all in the context of the underworld), we can do nothing but guess what the original names might have been.

It seems to me that Saxo cared a good deal about what were, for him, the old ways and the old stories. Enough to write them down so that they would be preserved for many more centuries. And enough to put them into a form where they would be held safely for a long time within what was, no doubt, the safest and longest lasting institution he knew: the church. I hope that this book will raise interest in some of these less appreciated Norse myths and legends.

* * *

HOTHER, NANNA, and BALDER

When Hother was young, he was fostered at King Gewar's court. Gewar had a daughter of a similar age to Hother, and she was called Nanna. Hother grew up to be strong and fast and wise, and he was skilled in archery and wrestling and swimming. Even when he was a young man, he was a formidable opponent, as he was so brave and determined. He was also a very good musician, and he could play the harp and the lyre and any other stringed instrument. And through his music, he could fill the hearts of those who heard him with joy or sadness, pity or hatred, delight or horror, whichever he wanted. Nanna fell very much in love with this fine young man.

There was a certain demigod called Balder. He was Odin's son. One time, Balder happened to be out walking close to Gewar's house, and he came to a place in the river where people would come to bathe. Balder saw Nanna while she was naked in the water, and he was overcome with desire. He decided at that moment that he must marry this girl. He would not let anything stand in his way. And if Nanna's love for Hother might make things difficult for him, then Hother must die.

Not long after that, Hother was out hunting when a strange mist swept in and surrounded him. The mist was thick, and he could barely see where he was going. He found himself among trees, and soon he came to a small wooden house. Hother left his horse outside, and he went in. There were three wood maidens in the house.

"Hail, Hother," the wood maidens said.

"Who are you?" Hother asked the maidens, "or how do you know my name?"

"We are governors of fortune," the maidens told him. "We can determine the fate of men. Some we favour, and we may bring them good fortune in battle. Others we may choose to destroy."

"We know that you have a problem, though you may not yet know it yourself. Balder has fallen in love with Nanna and is determined to marry her. Now that you know this, you may want to kill Balder. But you should not attack him, as it will be difficult for you to beat a god."

As soon as the maidens had spoken these words, they flew up into the air. Then the house also disappeared, and the mist cleared. Hother found that the trees were gone, and that he was standing with his horse in the middle of a wide open field under a clear sky. Hother got onto his horse and rode back to Gewar's house, thinking about everything that had just happened and what the maidens had said.

* * *

As soon as he got home, Hother went to speak to his fosterfather, King Gewar. He told him about everything that had happened to him that day, and what the wood maidens had told him, and he also asked him for Nanna's hand.

Gewar said: "I would be very happy to see you marry Nanna, but Balder has already asked for her hand, and I am afraid to refuse him.

"It will be difficult for you to fight against Balder," Gewar went on. "His skin is as hard as horn, and steel will not bite into him. But I know of a dwarf who can help you. That dwarf is called Mimming. He has some things that will be useful for you. The first is a sword of steel so hard and sharp that it cannot be beaten. The second is a golden ring with magical powers: it continually increases the wealth of the one who wears it. The dwarf keeps these things well guarded, but if you take them from him, you will find fortune in battle and also fortune in wealth.

"I will tell you where you can find this dwarf, Mimming," Gewar continued. "But it is not an easy journey. You must go north. You will find that the ground is covered in snow for most of the way, and it is very cold there. You should take a sledge with reindeer to pull it as those animals can easily move across snowy ground.

"The dwarf lives underground. When you find the entrance to the cave, you should put up your tent there and wait for the dwarf to come out. But be careful that your tent does not cast a shadow over the cave entrance. If Mimming sees a shadow, he will not come out. Instead, you should put up your tent so that the hill where the cave is casts a shadow onto the tent. Then you will see the dwarf when he comes out."

So Hother did as Gewar had said. He went off to the faraway north and crossed frozen wildernesses and snow-covered mountains. With the help of the reindeer he took with him, he was able to pass over drifted snow and icy wastes. The journey was long, but at last he came to the place where Mimming was, and he saw the entrance to the cave. Hother put up his tent outside the cave, and he made sure the tent did not cast a shadow over the entrance. Then Hother got into the tent and he waited.

A long time passed. By night, Hother stayed awake to continue his watch. By day he hunted for food to feed himself.

One time, Hother was keeping watch by night. He was very tired from having been awake for so long. Then suddenly he saw a shadow moving on the tent. It was the dwarf. Hother leapt up and flung his spear, and he knocked the dwarf over. He then rushed over and tied the dwarf up tightly so that he could not escape.

"Are you Mimming?" Hother said.

"Why do you want to know, or who are you?" the dwarf replied.

"I have come a long way to visit you. There are two things I came here for. The first is a sword, so hard and sharp that it cannot be beaten. The second is a gold ring that will make the one who wears it very rich. You will give me both of these things or it will cost your life."

Mimming was not slow to agree to this as he was very afraid. So Hother got the sword and the ring, and he was able to return home with these things by the same way he had come.

* * *

There was a King of Saxony who was called Gelder. Gelder heard that Hother had brought the sword and the ring from the north. He had heard all about these treasures, and he wanted them for himself, so he decided to attack.

Hother's fosterfather Gewar was skilled in the arts of prophecy and divining, so he saw what was about to happen, and he went to warn Hother.

"Gelder will come with a fleet of ships and attack you at sea," Gewar said to Hother. But it will be easy for you to beat him in battle if you follow my advice. Let him attack first. Wait, and be patient. Let his men throw all their spears, and don't throw any of your own until you see that they have none left. You should also take curved scythes that you can use to pull shields away from their men and also to damage their ships."

It was not long before Gelder's ships attacked, and when this happened Hother followed Gewar's advice.

Hother spoke to his men. "We will win this battle through patience," he said. "Do not rush in. Do not throw your spears. Form a shield wall and let them throw their spears until they have none left. That way we will win victory."

So Hother's men made an interlocking wall of their shields to protect themselves, and they waited as their enemies flung their spears. Gelder's men were eager to fight. They did not hold anything back. When they saw that Hother's men were reluctant to fight back, they threw their spears all the more eagerly, and soon they had none left.

When Gelder saw that he had no spears left and that Hother's men had not yet begun to attack, he realised that he would surely lose the battle. He quickly raised a red shield up to the top of the ship's mast as a signal of surrender. He hoped that his life might be spared.

So Hother was able to defeat Gelder more by gentleness than by strength, and more by cunning than by force. He greeted Gelder with a friendly face and kind words, and in this way he made his enemy into an ally.

* * *

While Hother was away one time, Balder came again to Gewar and asked him for Nanna's hand.

"You should go and speak to her," Gewar told him. "I will not allow any man to marry my daughter unless she agrees to it herself."

So Balder went to see Nanna. But no matter what he said to her, she would not be persuaded.

"It is not a good idea for us to get married," Nanna said to him. "You are a god and I am a mortal woman. Two people who are so different in nature should not get married. A god and a mortal could never be considered equals, and so a marriage between them could never work well.

"There will never be trust between people of such different backgrounds. Rich and poor keep apart from one another, and a promise given by one is hardly valued by the other. The rich have little regard for the fortunes of the poor. Why should the gods keep their promises to mortal men?

"No earthly creature could ever marry a god, as the gulf that keeps them apart is too great to cross. Mortals are nothing compared to the glory of the gods."

And so Balder left with nothing.

* * *

Gewar told Hother what had happened between Nanna and Balder, and Hother spoke to his father Helgi about it. But none of them could decide what to do about the situation. Even though it may bring comfort to a man to talk to his friends about his problems, it does not make those problems disappear. And so a stalemate had been reached. Neither Hother nor Balder was able to marry Nanna, and so the only way left to decide the thing was through bravery in battle. So they fought. And this was truly a battle of men against gods, as Odin and Thor and many others fought alongside Balder.

Hother had been given a coat that was protected by magic so that steel could not bite into it. He put on this coat and rushed forward on the battlefield. He attacked the gods fearlessly, even though he was only a mortal man.

Thor was swinging his club and crushing any man who came close. Every shield the club struck shattered, and no helmet was hard enough to withstand its strength. Thor stood alone, and was able to fight with no help from his allies. He called out and taunted his enemies, challenging them to come and attack him. It was difficult to see how the gods could lose the battle.

But then Hother ran to Thor, and taking him by surprise, he cut through the handle of the club with his sword. So Thor's club lost its handle, and it was useless after that.

When the gods saw what had happened to Thor's club, they grew afraid. Balder's army flew into disarray, and many of them fled, including Balder himself. Hother's men chased the enemy ships as they sailed away, and they killed as many as they could. Many ships sank in the sea, but Balder escaped.

One of those who died in the battle was King Gelder, who had been fighting alongside Hother. He was given a great funeral, fit for a king. He was laid on top of a pyre made from the bodies of his men, and his body was burned on one of his ships. After that his ashes were put into a barrow.

After this great victory of men over the gods, Hother returned to Gewar's house. And so it was that Hother and Nanna were able to get married at last. Balder was mocked about this disgraceful defeat for a long time after that.

* * *

For notes, see page 154

The DEATH of BALDER

Balder was disgraced by his defeat at the hands of Hother. He heard about Hother's marriage to Nanna, and soon after this he started to be troubled by terrible dreams. It was the figure of Nanna that haunted him, and now that he knew he would never have her he felt only anguish whenever she appeared. Whenever he slept he dreamed about her. When he was awake he got no rest. Balder's health began to suffer, and soon he had grown so unwell that he could no longer walk, and could only travel around by carriage.

Frustrated and powerless, Balder decided to attack his enemy. So he gathered his troops and took Hother by surprise. Hother was unprepared for such an attack, and was easily beaten. But Hother was not killed in the battle, and he fled back to Gewar's house.

After his victory, Balder saw that his men were tired and thirsty. So for their sake, he struck the earth at the place where they were standing. Streams of water sprang forth, and the men were able to drink.

But the victory hardly helped Balder. It might even have made things worse for him. For even though he had defeated Hother, he did not win Nanna, and he was tormented all the more.

Hother was also upset at this outcome. He was not pleased that he had been unable to repeat his earlier feat and defeat Balder for a second time. So Hother gathered his troops and attacked Balder, and they fought another battle. Both sides fought fiercely, and it was not clear who had the upper hand. But after some time, Hother sensed that he would be beaten, and he fled.

After this second defeat by Balder, Hother grew depressed. He felt that he no longer wanted to be around other people. For often when men are upset, they prefer to be alone. They find that it does not help their state of mind to be with others. So he went away from his court, and went to live alone as a hermit. For often those who are troubled in their minds will reject a civilised life, and prefer to live like beasts.

Hother's people were unhappy that their king had deserted them. "Where has he gone, or when will he come back?" they asked. "Who will rule us now?" But no-one knew the answers.

Hother followed a long and winding road through faraway lands, through high fells and deep forests. One time he came to a cave in the forest, and when he went in, he found three wood maidens there. It was the same three that had helped him earlier.

"Hail Hother," they said.

And now Hother knew very well who the maidens were.

"Why have you come here?" the maidens asked him.

"Things are not going well for me," Hother said. "I defeated Balder, and won Nanna. But since then I have fought with Balder twice more, and both times I was beaten. I fear he will soon take everything from me. Things have hardly gone as well for me as you said."

One of the maidens spoke to Hother: "Things have not gone as badly for you as you seem to think. You should not forget the victory you won over your enemies, and the losses that you brought them."

Another spoke: "It is difficult for you to fight against a god, and you are right to fear Balder. He means to eat a certain magical meal that will increase his strength. If he eats that, it will be difficult for you to beat him. But if you eat it yourself, you will find that victory will come easily to you."

Encouraged by these words, Hother returned to his home and started to plan another attack on Balder.

The two armies gathered, and as night fell, Hother went walking to spy on the enemy camp. He met a man there, but the man didn't know who he was.

"Has anyone come to visit Balder?" Hother asked the man.

"Yes, three maidens came to cook for him," he answered.

"Tell me which way they went," Hother said.

"They came this way, but I don't know where they were going," the man said.

So Hother followed the footprints in the dew on the ground, and soon he came to a tent where the maidens were preparing food.

"Who are you?" one of them asked him when he went into the tent.

"I am a musician," said Hother. Of course he was telling the truth.

So he was given a lyre. Hother tuned the strings, and he began to play a pleasant tune. Everyone who heard it agreed that it was very good. As he played, he was able to see what the maidens were doing.

They were preparing the magic meal that they would give to Balder. There were three snakes hanging above the cooking pot, and venom was dripping from their open jaws into the food as the maidens stirred it.

Hother spoke to the maidens. "Is this the food that will give strength?" he asked them.

"It is," they said.

Hother asked them whether he might eat the food. Two of the maidens wanted to give him some, but the eldest of them overruled them and forbade it. "We made this food for Balder," she said. "It would not be right to give it to his enemy."

But then the maidens gave Hother a belt.

"If you wear this belt you will not be beaten," they said to him.

So Hother put on the belt and he left the house.

While he was on his way back to his own camp, he saw Balder walking to the place he had just come from. Hother struck with his sword and he gave Balder a terrible wound. Then he left him on the ground to die.

But Balder did not die at once, even though the wound was very bad. The next morning, the armies met. Hother's men were encouraged when they heard that Balder had been badly injured. But although he could not walk, and although the wound was very painful, Balder had his men carry him onto the battlefield, so that everyone might see that he was still alive. Both sides fought fiercely, and the battle was not decided that day.

When night came, Balder dreamed a dreadful dream. He saw Hel come to him in his dream. She told him that he would soon be in her arms, and he knew that he would die the next day.

And so it happened. Balder died of the wound that Hother had given him. He was given a great funeral, and then his body was buried in a barrow.

One time, grave robbers went to that barrow meaning to take whatever treasures they could find there, for they were sure that Balder would have been buried with many valuable things. But as they approached, a roaring torrent of water sprang forth from the mound. The fast-flowing stream engulfed all that it encountered as it rushed downhill. When they saw this, the grave robbers dropped their tools and fled. After this spring appeared, no-one else dared to disturb Balder's barrow.

* * *

For notes, see page 154

VENGEANCE for BALDER

When Odin heard about what had happened to Balder, he was very upset. He swore that his son would be avenged, and he consulted a number of seeresses and other oracles to try to determine how this might happen.

One of these was a Finn called Rostoff, who said this to Odin: "No-one has been born who will avenge Balder."

Odin was not pleased to hear this, but the oracle continued: "Balder will be avenged by his brother, your son. The mother of this child will be called Rinda, who is the daughter of the king of Russia."

When Odin heard this, he travelled to Russia at once, and went in to see the king. He pulled his hat down over his face so that he would not be recognised.

"Who are you, or what do you want?" asked the king.

"I have come a long way to serve you," said Odin.

The king agreed that he could stay, and he gave him a number of men to command. Odin fought in a battle for the king, and won a great victory. After that, the king regarded him very highly, and gave him many gifts and honours.

Not long after that, Odin went out alone, and killed a whole army of the king's enemies. It was amazing to think that one man could singlehandedly destroy so many armed men. No-one could understand how he had done it.

The king was very pleased with the service Odin gave him. Finally, Odin revealed to the king that he was in love with his daughter, Rinda, and he asked whether he could marry her.

The king was pleased to hear this. "You should go up and speak to her about that yourself," he said.

So Odin went to Rinda's chamber. But when she heard his proposal, instead of a kiss she gave him a slap. And Odin had to leave with nothing.

But Odin did not give up easily, and he was not discouraged by the girl's refusal. One year later, he disguised himself again. He dressed himself in foreign clothes and covered himself in soot and grime, and he returned to the king's court.

"Who are you, or why have you come here?" asked the king.

"My name is Roster, and I am a smith," said Odin.

So Odin went to work as a smith in the king's smithy. First he worked in bronze, and he made many beautiful objects. Everything was so well made that when the king saw it he sent a lot of gold to Roster, and told him to make jewellery for the ladies.

Odin made many precious things from that gold for the ladies to wear, and then he went on to work on some beautiful ornaments as gifts for Rinda. He made a ring for her, and put more work and care into polishing and finishing it than any of the other things he had made. Then he made several more rings, and he put as much work into each of those.

He took the rings to the girl, and presented them to her. But she was very angry, and she gave him a slap. She was not pleased to be given such wonderful gifts by the old smith. For so often, the true value of a gift depends on the giver. Gifts from a loved one are often gratefully received, while gifts from one we dislike are unwelcome, no matter what the gift itself might be. Rinda suspected that this smith would seize any chance he could to have her, and that these gifts were all part of his scheme. She was sure that his true wishes were hidden behind his pretence of generosity.

So Odin had to leave again. The king was not happy to hear that his daughter had refused this man.

But she told him: "I have no wish to marry such an old man while I am so young."

And the king had some sympathy with that.

Although Odin was not pleased that Rinda had rejected him again, he did not give up. He knew that girls could often be won by stubborn persistence. So he disguised himself a third time.

Odin was so skilled in magic that he could change his shape according to his will. He sensed that he might have more luck with Rinda if he appeared to be a younger and taller man. So he changed his appearance, and dressed as a warrior. He rode up to the king's house on horseback, and he challenged many of the kingdom's finest warriors to riding competitions.

Rinda was not impressed. Even though Odin now looked very different, she still disliked him very much. So when he went to her for a kiss, she pushed him away so hard that he fell over and banged his chin on the floor.

By now, Odin was angry with this stubborn girl. He carved magic runes on a piece of bark, and he touched her with it. Rinda lost her mind and became mad. Odin enjoyed his moment of revenge. And yet still he could not have her.

Odin did not give up. He was so confident in his own abilities that he did not think about failure at all, but only about what tactic he could use to get the result he wanted. So Odin dressed himself as a woman. And in this fourth disguise, he went to see the king for a fourth time.

"Who are you, or why have you come here?" the king asked.

"My name is Wecha," Odin said. "And I am a healer."

Most people believed that he was a woman because of the way he dressed. So Odin stayed with the women at court, and he became a maidservant to Rinda. He would wash Rinda's feet every evening, and he would also carefully wash her calves and the upper parts of her thighs with his hands.

Finally, Odin got a stroke of luck. Rinda fell ill, and the healing woman Wecha (which is to say Odin) was called upon to help her.

Wecha examined Rinda's body thoroughly, and then went to speak to her father.

"The girl is seriously ill," Wecha said. "There is a healing drink that I can give her. But I fear she will find it very bitter, and she will not swallow it unless she is tied down."

As soon as the king heard this, he went in to his daughter at once and tied her to the bed. "Do whatever Wecha tells you to do," he told her. And then the king left them alone.

The so-called healer saw his opportunity, and he was finally able to have his way with the girl. Weakened by illness, and tied to the bed by her father, Rinda was unable to resist. And so she was forced to submit to what she had rejected for so long when she was in good health.

There are those that say that the king saw the old man leaning over his daughter, breathing hard and moaning in the course of his so-called healing duties, and yet he did nothing. They say the king regretted his inaction later when Rinda gave birth to a baby boy.

* * *

Rinda's son was called Boe. When he had grown up, he challenged Hother in battle. Hother had been warned in prophecies and by the visions of seers that he would die in this battle, and that is what happened. Hother was killed. But Boe did not live long to enjoy his victory. He was badly wounded in the fight, and he could not walk off the battlefield. He had to be lifted up onto a shield and carried by his men.

Boe died of his wound the next day. He was given a magnificent funeral, and his body was buried in a barrow. This great warrior was remembered for a long time after that.

* * *

For notes, see page 154

ODIN's DISGRACE and EXILE (1)

When the other gods heard what Odin had done with Rinda, they were outraged. The things they found the most disgraceful were that he had taken the form of a woman, and that he had used a certain form of magic. They were disgusted by what had happened, and they feared that their own reputation would be ruined by their association with Odin. They thought that if they did nothing, it could lead to all their deaths, and so they felt they had to act.

So Odin was removed from his position as chief of the gods. They made him an outlaw and sent him into exile.

Another god was chosen to take Odin's place as the leader of the gods. His name was Oller. But when he became the chief of the gods, he also took Odin's name so that there would be no confusion, and everyone called him by that name.

Many years passed, and Odin lived in filth and dirt in the wilderness. But he was not forgotten, and after some time, some of the gods began to suggest that he had suffered enough, and that he should be allowed to return. When the gods heard others speaking on his behalf, they started to feel sorry for Odin, and more were convinced that he should be invited back.

So Odin returned to the glorious old halls where he had ruled before. He took back his powers and resumed his old life, and his glory shone bright again across the land.

It seems that the passage of time acted in Odin's favour, and the terrible things he had done were forgotten. But there were also those who did not forget, and who thought that Odin was unworthy of his former position. Some believe that Odin paid some of the gods to speak on his behalf with expensive gifts of gold.

When Odin returned, he banished Oller from Asgard. Oller could travel over the water by using a certain magic. He had a bone that was inscribed with runes. Using this bone, he was able to cross the sea without a boat, and to travel over any water that barred his way as quickly as if he was rowing. Oller was forced to flee to Sweden, and there he was attacked and killed.

* * *

For notes, see page 157

The GODS and the GIANTS

There are three sorts of supernatural beings you should know about.

The first are the giants. These are huge creatures, much bigger than men, and they are strong and powerful.

The second call themselves gods. These beings are skilled in magic, and gifted with the art of prophecy. They are much wiser than the giants, but not as big, and not as strong. Many wars were fought between the giants and these gods, but ultimately the giants were beaten, and the gods became the ruling masters.

Both these groups are shapeshifters. They can change their appearance to hide their true form. But they can do more than this: using their magical powers they can even change the shape of the world around them.

The third group also call themselves gods. These are the offspring of unions between the giants and the other gods. But they inherited little of any worth from their parents. They lack the size of the giants, and their magical skills are weak. These gods rely on trickery to keep themselves in their positions of power.

* * *

For notes, see page 158

ODIN's DISGRACE and EXILE (2)

Some say that Odin's disgrace and exile came about in quite a different way, and that it all started with a golden statue.

Odin had a statue of himself set up. It was a very good likeness, and he was very pleased with it. The whole statue was covered in shining gold, and it had also been given precious gold arm rings to wear on its golden arms.

Odin's wife Frigg did not like this statue at all. But she liked the gold that covered it very much. She wanted that gold for herself. She wanted to have the gold made into jewellery that she could wear to make herself even more beautiful. So Frigg went to see some smiths.

"You should strip all the gold off Odin's statue," she said. "Melt it down and bring it to me, and you will be rewarded."

The smiths did as they were told, but Odin was very angry when he found out what happened. And things turned out badly for those smiths. They paid with their lives for what they had done.

Odin then set the statue up on a pedestal and gave it magical powers so that it could speak.

When she saw that Odin had set up his statue again, Frigg grew very angry, and she was determined to pay him back. So she spoke to one of her serving men: "You should break that statue down," she said to him. "And then come and visit me in my chamber this evening."

So that man did as he was told. He came to visit Frigg, and they spent the night together.

Soon all the gods knew what had happened. It was very shameful for Odin that his wife had slept with another man of such low status, and also that she had destroyed the statue made in his image. Odin's disgrace was so great that he had to leave his position as the leader of the gods, and he went into exile.

While Odin was away, there was another who took his place as leader of the gods. He called himself Mid-Odin, so he took Odin's name as well as his position and privileges.

Odin spent many years in the wilderness. But then news reached him that Frigg had died. Everyone forgot about the shame that Frigg had brought upon Odin, and the glory of his name was restored. He returned after that to his former halls, and he drove out those who had tried to replace him.

Mid-Odin was outlawed, and was forced to flee to Finland, and there he was attacked and killed. His body was buried in a barrow, and he haunted that barrow for a long time after that. Anyone who went near that barrow soon died.

* * *

For notes, see page 157

THORKILL's JOURNEY to VISIT GEIRROD

There was once a king called Gorm. He was thought of as a great king, but this was not due to his victories in battle or success in war. Gorm was renowned for his feats of exploration. He longed for new knowledge. Whenever he heard stories about extraordinary things in faraway places, he always wanted to travel to see these wonders with his own eyes.

One day a man called Thorkill came to Gorm's court. This is what Thorkill said to the king: "I know of a land in the faraway north where a certain Geirrod lives. There are great piles of gold there. But the journey to that land is very long and filled with dangers, and it is difficult for any man to make it there alive. First you must sail on the sea for so long that you leave the sun and the stars behind. Then you pass into chaos. From there you must journey further into a land of darkness where there is no light at all."

Gorm was very pleased when he heard this. "I want to visit this Geirrod," he said. "It matters little to me whether or not there is treasure there to be had. The journey will be worth making for its own sake. There will be glory to be won simply by finding such an inaccessible place. I will take three hundred men with me. You know the way there, Thorkill, so you will guide us."

Thorkill agreed to this. "But the seas will be very rough," he said. "First we should build three new ships, big and strong. Each one will hold a hundred men. The ships should be nailed with many nails and tied with many ropes. The top side of the ships should be covered in oxhides to prevent the spray of breaking waves from coming in. And the ships should be loaded with plenty of food and provisions."

So three new ships were built just as Thorkill had said, and then they all set sail.

They sailed northwards on fair winds as far as Halogaland, but then the winds changed. The wind buffeted the seas and tossed the ships among the waves. They were blown off course, and after a while, the food supplies began to run low. Even the bread was finished.

The men grew desperate. But then they heard a sound that could have been the crash of thunder or the sound of waves breaking against rocks. Thorkill spoke to a little small boy: "You boy, climb the mast and see what you can see."

So the boy climbed the mast, and he cried out: "I can see an island in the distance, steep and rocky."

The men were heartened by this, and with renewed strength they rowed as hard as they could towards the place where the island lay.

It was late in the afternoon when they reached the shore. Leaving the ships on the beach, the men climbed up through the rocks and past the high cliffs until they came to a flat grassy plain. There were crowds of cattle in that place. Those cattle were not shy or fearful. They did not run away from the men. Instead, they were inquisitive and came close, so it was very easy for the men to catch them.

Thorkill said: "Only take as many cattle as you need to satisfy your hunger. I fear that if we kill more, the spirits in this place will not be pleased."

But the men didn't listen to Thorkill's words. They caught and killed many cattle. They had a great feast that evening, and they loaded the carcases of many more uneaten cattle onto the ships.

Late that night, the men were woken from their sleep by a dreadful noise from the island. First there were terrible cries from the darkness beyond the cliffs. Then they saw a giant with a huge rough-hewn club rushing down through the rocks towards the beach, and many smaller trolls with him.

The giant stood in the water and cried out to them in a terrible voice: "You have killed many cattle from the herd of the gods, and you will pay for this. I will have the lives of one man from each of your three ships, or none of you will ever leave this place."

Thorkill spoke to the king: "It would be better to give this giant what he asks for so that the rest of us might come away from here."

The king agreed, and so the men drew lots. The three who were chosen were sent out to the trolls on the beach, and then the three ships set sail as quickly as they could and continued on their way.

A fair wind took them to a land called Bjarmeland, which is covered in ice and snow, even in the summer. That land is covered by a great forest, wild and pathless. Few people live there, and there are no fields of corn or other crops. The rivers and streams that flow through that forest all run white with spray and foam as they crash and splash through the rocks. There are also many strange animals living in that forest.

Thorkill said: "We should land here. It will not be far for us to reach Geirrod now. But if we should meet anyone in this land, you should not speak a word to them. Let me talk to them, or things could turn out badly."

So they landed and put up their tents on the beach. Later that same day, the men were shocked to see a giant approaching their camp. The giant walked up to them and greeted the men in friendly tones, and spoke to many of them, but they all remained silent.

Then Thorkill spoke to the men: "This giant is called Gudmund, and his house is not far from here. He is Geirrod's brother. You should not fear him as he doesn't mean to harm you. He welcomes any travellers who come this way."

"Why do these men not speak?" Gudmund asked Thorkill.

"It is because they don't speak your language well, and they are ashamed to try," Thorkill said.

Gudmund was satisfied with this answer, and he said: "You must all come to visit me at my house and be my guests."

So the men got into carriages that Gudmund had brought, and they followed the giant in the direction of his house. As they went, they passed alongside a dark river, very wide, and there was a golden bridge that crossed the river.

"Can we not go across that bridge?" some of the men asked.

But Gudmund said: "This river divides the world of men from the world of monsters. It is forbidden for any living man to cross that bridge."

So they continued on their way. Then Thorkill said to the men: "While we are at Gudmund's house you should not eat any of the food that is offered to you, and do not drink any of the drink. If anyone you meet there should speak to you, you should not say anything in reply. You may be sorely tempted, but you should resist the temptation for your own safety. If you eat the food or drink the drink that Gudmund offers, you will certainly lose your minds. You will forget everything about your former lives, you will be bewitched, and you will not be able to leave this place again."

They soon arrived at Gudmund's house, and the men went into the hall. It was a magnificent building. Gudmund's twelve noble sons were there, and also his twelve beautiful daughters. Servants brought out food and drink and offered it to Gorm's men, but the men didn't eat it. They had brought their own food with them, and they only ate that.

When Gudmund saw that the men were not eating his food or drinking his drink, he was upset, and he said to Thorkill: "Why are these men not eating my food? This is good food that I am offering to you all as my guests."

Thorkill said: "Often when men travel to foreign lands, it can be bad for them to eat the local food. Unfamiliar food can be disagreeable to them or make them feel ill, even though the local people enjoy that food very much. These men are simply looking after their own health, and that is why they are eating the food they have brought with them themselves."

Gudmund could not argue with this answer. But when he saw that he would be unable to tempt the men with food, he tried to persuade them in other ways.

So Gudmund said to King Gorm: "I offer you my daughter's hand in marriage." And to the king's men he said: "You may have whichever women you want from my household."

Many men were tempted, but most of them remembered Thorkill's warning and refused. It was a difficult job for Thorkill to persuade the men to refuse all that was offered while also thinking of words to say to their generous host so that he would not be offended. Four of the men decided that they would rather take their chances with the local women. Those men lost their minds at once. They could never leave that place, and they lost their chance to return as heroes to their own country.

But Gudmund had plans to lure more of the men. He said to King Gorm: "Will you not come out to the garden with me? I would like to show you the pretty flowers that grow there, and I am sure you would like to taste the different fruits and berries that you will find on the bushes and trees."

Thorkill said to Gudmund: "You are very kind, but it is important that we go on our way. It is a shame that there is no time to visit your garden now, but we have lingered here too long already."

Gudmund saw then that he was not going to be able to persuade more of the men to stay with him, and he gave up. "If you are determined that you will go on your way," he said, "then you must go."

And so Gudmund ferried them all across the river, and they entered the land where Geirrod was.

On they went, and further on, through that desolate land and across a dark and featureless plain. At last, a walled town rose up in front of them. The place looked as though it was in ruins, though they could barely see it as the light was bad, and it was also surrounded by a thick cloud of smoke. On top of the wall that surrounded the town was a fence built of wooden staves, and on top of each of these staves was a dead man's head.

"This is the place," said Thorkill.

The gate to enter into this town was high above them, and it could only be reached by a ladder. But at the bottom of the ladder, fierce dogs snarled and growled. Thorkill threw a bone covered in greasy flesh to those dogs, and while they were distracted, the men climbed the ladder and entered into the town.

The place was filled with filth and decay, and there was an overpowering stench that was quite unbearable. Dark spirits walked in the streets, and although they were terrible to look at, the sound of their shrieking voices tormented the men even more.

They soon reached a rocky place. "This is Geirrod's hall," said Thorkill to the men. "You should not be afraid to go in, but listen to my words. In these halls, you will see many things, some of them terrible, some of them wonderful. Do not fear any of the terrible things you may see. But you must remember this. Do not touch any of the treasures you may see, no matter how much you may want them, and no matter how much they may tempt you. If you grasp hold of what you cannot have, your hands may be stuck fast, and it will be hard for you to leave this place."

And so they went in. Two of the bravest men, called Buck and Broder, went first along with Thorkill and the king, and the others followed them. The sight that met them as they entered the first hall was not pleasant. The roof of that place was made of spears, and the dirty floor was covered in slithering snakes. The doorposts were covered in soot, and the walls were smeared with grime. The place was also in ruins, and the room was filled with a foul stench. All the men found it sickening to their eyes, noses, and minds.

Along the walls of that hall, there were iron benches, ornamented with lead, and trolls were sitting on these benches. There were more trolls in the middle of the hall, playing a game of tug-of-war with a goatskin. The trolls on the benches screamed in delight as they watched the spectacle. Grim porters stood in all the doorways.

Then they passed through into a second hall. The sight that met them was perhaps even worse. An old giant sat in the high seat at the end of the room with his chest pierced by an iron bar. Three more huge figures sat slumped in chairs next to him. Looking closely at them, it seemed that they were giantesses, but they were very ugly and deformed.

"What has happened here?" the men asked.

Thorkill explained it to them: "This is Geirrod. Long ago, this giant provoked Thor, and he was rewarded with a red-hot iron bar through the chest. His female companions were also punished with Thor's thunderbolts.

"Now we have seen Geirrod, we should go," Thorkill said.

But as they were leaving the room, some of the men spotted some treasures that were standing in one corner. There were seven barrels, all filled to the top with gold, and wrapped around with silver chains. Alongside were three more wonderful objects: a heavy golden arm-ring, the antler of a stag, inlaid with gold and precious stones, and the tusk of an enormous beast, covered in gold at both ends. Three of the men could not stop themselves. One reached out and took the ring, another grasped the antler, and a third took the tusk. None of them thought too much about what might happen, but things went worse for them than they had hoped.

At once, the ring turned into a snake that attacked the man who had taken it, killing him with its poisonous bite. Then the antler also turned into a snake, and it too killed the man who had taken it. The tusk turned into a sword, but the man could not control it. It was as though the sword could fight on its own without any hand holding it. The sword turned on the man and killed him. When the others saw what had happened, they feared for their lives, and they quickly left that room behind.

So they entered a third hall. In that hall, there were even more treasures laid out. There were weapons and armour and wonderful clothes that were so large that they were better suited to giants than men. There was a cloak of the kind worn by kings, all richly embroidered with fine patterns in silver and gold thread. And there was a helmet, and a belt covered in beautiful and detailed patterns.

When Thorkill saw these things, he was amazed. He forgot everything that he had said to the men. He was overcome by his desire to take these beautiful things for himself. So he picked up the cloak and took it.

When the men saw Thorkill do this, they restrained themselves no longer, but eagerly helped themselves to as many of the precious things that they could get their hands on. But as they laid their hands on the treasures, the room began to tremble and shake, and there came a terrible cry from another room, hideous to hear.

"Thieves," the voices screamed. "Stop them!" It was the women who had sat slumped in silence who now cried out. Those giantesses had not been dead as they had seemed.

When they heard the cry, the trolls who had sat huddled and motionless along the walls all leapt up from their shadowy benches. They rushed to attack Thorkill and Gorm and the others, and many other trolls roared them on.

There was a great battle. The men fought fiercely, throwing spears and attacking with bows and arrows, but many of them were killed. Of all the men who had come with Gorm, only twenty came out of Geirrod's hall alive. Many trolls were killed as well, and the ones who killed the most trolls were Broder and Buck.

So Thorkill and Gorm and the few survivors left that town behind them and made their way back the way they had come across the desolate plain until they came to the river. Gudmund was waiting there for them and he ferried them across.

"You must come and stay with me awhile," Gudmund said to them. "Be my guests while you recover from your ordeal."

So they all went back to Gudmund's house, and again, Gudmund tried to tempt them with food and drink and women and other gifts. But he was frustrated when he saw that still they seemed able to resist the good things that he offered them.

All except for Buck. This man, who had shown such bravery in Geirrod's hall, and who had proved himself a great warrior in the battle against the trolls, gave in to temptation when he fell in love with one of Geirrod's daughters. He kissed her, and at once he lost his mind. His thoughts span, and his memories of his former life faded. The hero who had come through so much on this dangerous journey was overcome by his love for one girl.

Thorkill and Gorm and the other men left Gudmund's house to return to the ships. When Buck saw them leaving, he felt torn between his loyalty to the king and his sense the he must remain with his wife. He chased after the men, but when he came to a ford, his carriage sank in the mud at the bottom of the river, and Buck was washed away and drowned.

The king's voyage home was not straightforward. They sailed with fair winds in the beginning, but then the weather changed, and they found themselves blown off course. More of the men died of hunger, and the king was growing desperate. The men all had their own ideas about which god they should pray to for a fair wind. But Gorm prayed to Utgardaloki, and the weather improved.

And so with Thorkill as his guide, Gorm survived the journey to Geirrod's hall and back again. He sailed back across the sea to Denmark. But he was worn out by all that he had seen on his journey, and disheartened from losing so many men. So Gorm married a Swedish girl. He stayed at home and lived a quiet life after that.

* * *

For notes, see page 159

THORKILL's JOURNEY to UTGARD

After his return from Geirrod's land, King Gorm lived in peace and quiet for the rest of his life. But as he grew old, he started to worry about what might happen to him after his death. He thought about everything that he had done in his life, and wondered whether this might affect what happened to him.

There were men at Gorm's court who did not like Thorkill at all, and who wished him nothing but ill. Those men went to the king, and they said this: "This matter is too great for men's minds to fathom, even though it is so important. A good answer to this question may only be found by speaking directly to the gods. You should send Thorkill to visit Utgardaloki to ask him about this matter that is troubling you. He is certainly the best man for this. If he returns, you will get your answer. If he dies on this mission, it will be no loss for you as Thorkill is no friend of yours."

So the king called Thorkill to him, and told him what he wanted him to do.

Thorkill could not refuse, although the journey was very dangerous, and he had no wish to go. "I will do this," he said to the king. "But those men who told you to send me to visit Utgardaloki should sail with me."

When they heard this, the men were terrified, and they tried to refuse.

"Are you cowards, then?" the king asked them.

And so they had to agree to sail with Thorkill.

They started to make preparations for the voyage. "The ship should be loaded with plenty of provisions," said Thorkill. "And the top part should be covered with oxhide to prevent the sea spray from coming in."

And so they set sail. They sailed for a long time, and they left the sun and the stars behind and entered a land of shadows and everlasting night. They sailed further on, and after some time they ran out of firewood so they had no way of cooking their meat. They had to eat it raw. Many of the men who ate the raw meat became ill. The sickness spread from their bellies throughout their bodies, and many of them died. So it was dangerous to eat, but those who did not eat grew weaker.

But as they reached the depths of despair, there came a glimmer of hope through the darkness. Thorkill spotted the flicker of firelight on the shore. "We should land here," he told the men. "And I will go and see whether I can fetch some fire."

So the ship came into the shore. Thorkill attached a gemstone to the top of the mast so that by its shine he might find his way back to the ship. And then he went off in the direction of the smoke and sparks.

Thorkill followed a narrow path through the rocks, and he entered a cave. It was a disgusting place. There was mould on the walls, the roof was stained with dirt and grime, and the floor swarmed with snakes. In the middle of the cave, giants were sitting by the side of a fire. Those giants were very ugly, with huge noses.

One of the giants spoke: "Who are you who has come walking in the darkness, or why have you come here?"

Thorkill said: "I have come on a long journey with my companions. We are searching for Utgardaloki, and I have come to you to ask the way."

"It is a strange thing to try to go beyond the end of the world," said the giant, "and it is hard to visit the gods and then return. I can help you with what you ask. But first you should tell me three true facts."

"I can do that for you," said Thorkill. "First, my eyes have never seen uglier trolls than you, or bigger noses. Second, I can think of no worse place for me to live than here. Third, my best foot is the one that steps forward first to leave this place."

"That was well said," said the giant. "Now I will tell you what you want to know. You should row for four days and four nights without stopping, and then you will reach a dark land where nothing grows.

You will find many caves there, filthy and ugly, and in one of those caves you will find Utgardaloki."

Thorkill was not pleased to hear that the journey was still long, and that the conditions would not improve.

"I have one more thing to ask of you," he said to the giants. "Can I take some fire from you?"

"Of course you can take some fire," said the giant. "But first you should tell me another three true facts."

"Yes I can do that," said Thorkill. "First, good advice should always be followed, even if it was given by a bad man. Second, I was careless to come here, and if I come out alive I will have my legs to thank for it. And third, I will never come here again."

The giants were satisfied with this, and Thorkill returned to the ship with the fire. The flicker of the gemstone on the mast showed him which way to go. And finally the men were able to cook and eat.

So they set sail again, and on the fourth day they came to that dark land where they were headed. There was no day or night there, only darkness. They left the ship and walked inland. And before long they reached a cliff, though they could hardly see it until it was right in front of them as it was so dark.

"This must be the place," said Thorkill. "We should go into this cave, but light a fire here at the entrance to ward off any dark spirits that might come this way."

So Thorkill and the men went into the cave. They carried torches so they could see, but the sight that met their eyes was not a pleasant one. There were many iron seats in the cave, and the floor was covered in slithering snakes.

At the back of the cave, a stream was flowing over a sandy bed. They crossed this stream, and then they saw that the cave extended downwards. So they followed the passageway deeper and further in, until they came to a huge inner chamber, ugly and dark. A giant was sitting in the middle of the room, bound hand and foot with heavy chains. It was Utgardaloki himself.

Thorkill wanted some proof that he had been there, so he went up to the sleeping giant, and plucked one of the hairs from his chin. That hair was as big as a spear shaft, and just as stiff. But it also reeked with such a foul stench that none of them would have been able to breathe if they had not covered their noses with their cloaks.

As the men tried to leave, they were attacked by snakes. They slithered in from every direction, spitting their poison. Some even flew overhead and spat poison at the men from above. The men protected themselves using their cloaks.

One man failed to cover his arm, and when the poison hit it, the arm withered and came off at the shoulder. Another man looked out from under his cloak. Poison hit his eyes, and he was blinded at once. Another man put his head out from under the cloak. Poison hit him, and his head came off at the neck as though it had been sliced by a sword.

Of all the men that had come with Thorkill, only five made it out of there alive. They hurried back to the ship, and set sail for home.

The stench of the hair that Thorkill had taken from Utgardaloki's chin was too much for some of the men. They couldn't stand the bad air that they were forced to breathe, and some of them also died. Only two men made it back with Thorkill.

* * *

News that Thorkill had returned reached the king, and the king was keen to speak to him. But then some men said this to him: "Have you not heard, king, that if you hear what Thorkill has to say to you, and you let him tell you what he has seen, then it will mean your death?"

And it was true that Gorm had foreseen in a dream that Thorkill would tell him terrible things that he had learned on his journey to Utgard, and that he would die soon afterwards. So Gorm became afraid. He didn't want to see Thorkill, and he ordered his men to put Thorkill to death as he slept in his bed.

But Thorkill heard what the king was planning, and he put a log in his bed. He watched the king's men come into his house and attack the log with swords and axes.

Then Thorkill went to the king. "I have served you faithfully all my life," he said, "and I have put myself in great danger for your sake. But now rather than thanking me, or even hearing what I have to tell you about what I have seen, you try to have me killed in my sleep."

Then Thorkill told the king everything that had happened. He brought out the hair that he had plucked from Utgardaloki's chin.

Several people who were there breathed in the stench from that hair and died.

The king could not bear to hear Thorkill's description of Utgardaloki held imprisoned in that place, filthy and suffering. So not long after Thorkill left him, King Gorm killed himself.

* * *

For notes, see page 159

SYRITHA and OTTAR

There was once a king's daughter called Syritha. She was very beautiful, and many men wanted to marry her. But this girl was determined that she would not even look at any of them.

She thought that if she allowed her eyes to look at a man, she may be overcome by temptation and lust for what she saw, and give in to her desires. She said this to her father: "I will only raise my eyes and look at a man if he can persuade me to do so by the words that he speaks. If any man persuades me to do this, then that is the man I will marry."

Many men came to visit this girl, and they said many things to her. But all the time, Syritha gazed at her own feet. She never lifted her eyes to look at any of the men who had come.

There was a young man called Ottar who had heard about Syritha, and he went to visit her. He was sure that he would be able to persuade her to look at him, as he had already done many great deeds. But no matter what he said, she did not look up. She only stared at the ground. Ottar was impressed by the girl's willpower, but he had to leave with nothing.

There was a certain giant who had also heard about Syritha, and he was very interested in this girl. But when he went to see her, she also refused to look at him. So the giant had to leave. When he had gone away, that giant thought of a plan whereby he might take her away for himself. The giant cut out and sewed women's clothes for himself, and dressed himself as a woman. Then he went knocking on Syritha's door.

"Who are you, or what do you want?"

This is what the giant said: "I am just a maiden who has come from a faraway land. I have come here to spin and sew, and to serve you, maiden. Open the door."

And the giant was let in.

One day, Syritha went out walking with the new maidservant (which is to say the giant). They walked further than Syritha usually went, far from her father's house, and out towards the mountains.

"Maybe we should turn back," said Syritha.

But the maidservant (or the giant) said: "I know this road very well."

And they kept walking. When Syritha grew so tired that she could no longer walk, the maidservant (or the giant) picked her up and carried her. But that giant did not carry her back to her own home. He carried her to a place surrounded by rocks, high on a mountain ledge, difficult to reach and even harder to find.

The news travelled that Syritha had been taken away to the mountains by a giant, and when Ottar heard this, he grew determined that he should go and find her. "Then she will surely look at me," he said.

So Ottar wandered in the wilderness for a long time. He walked among huge rocks and under the shadows of high cliffs, but it was hard to find anything in those desolate mountains. Then one evening as he was walking, he saw smoke rising from a place high above him, and saw the flicker of firelight among the dark cliffs. He knew then that he had found the place, and he climbed higher and higher until he reached it.

When the giant saw Ottar, he said to him: "Who are you who comes here so late at night?"

Ottar said: "I have come looking for the maiden Syritha, and I see that now at last I have found her here."

Then Ottar rushed in and slew the giant. But Ottar found that the giant had knotted Syritha's long golden hair in such a way that she couldn't go free. The knotted and matted hair could not be untied. So Ottar had to cut it all off the girl's head. And in this way he was able to free her.

And yet still Syritha would not lift her eyes to look at Ottar. No matter what he said to her, she gazed at the ground.

Of course, Ottar was very disappointed with this result. After a while, he gave up. He left Syritha in the mountains, and he returned home himself.

Syritha wandered in the mountains, along winding paths through desolate lands, unsure of where she was going. While she was walking in the woods, she came to a hut where a giantess lived.

"You, girl, can look after my goats," the giantess said to her. And that is what Syritha did.

News came to Ottar that Syritha was working as a goatherdess for a giant woman. He thought that it was a disgrace that such a noble girl should find herself in this situation, and he resolved to go and rescue her a second time. He thought as well that if he did this it might count in his favour with Syritha.

Ottar came to the place where the giantess lived, and he found Syritha there with the goats. He spoke this verse to her:

I will take you, away from these goats,
And your miserable mistress.
For so long, I have longed for you,
Now take me into your arms.

For many months, I have searched for you,
So look at me now, maiden.
I will take you home, to your father's house,
Only look at me now, maiden.

Many times, I have saved you, maiden,
From the grip of giants.
Give your rescuer, a fair reward,
Lift up your eyes to me.

How can you choose, to live with giants,
And choose to do their chores?
How can you choose, to care for beasts,
And go with goats every day?

> Grant me now my great desire,
> Grant yourself your own desire,
> Come away and marry me!

But Syritha did not look up.

Ottar could not understand that Syritha would not even look at him. But he was also embarrassed and ashamed that he had wasted so much of his time and effort on this girl, and he regretted it very much. So he left Syritha and returned home.

Syritha wandered again for a long time in the wilderness. She was lost and alone. She walked for a long time among rocks and hills, and when at last she came to a house, she looked thin and bedraggled. She was dirty, and her fine clothes were torn so that all she had left were little more than rags. It happened that the house she had come to was Ottar's house, and the woman standing outside the house was Ottar's mother.

"Who are you, girl, or where have you come from," Ottar's mother asked her.

"I am no-one but a poor farmer's daughter," Syritha said. She knew very well how undressed she must look, and she was very ashamed of her appearance.

But Ottar's mother saw that the girl had a noble look about her, and she told her to come in and sit beside her in the high seat.

When Ottar returned home that evening, he was surprised to see Syritha sitting there beside his mother. He saw very well who it was who had come, though she looked at the floor and hid her face in her cloak.

"Why are you hiding your face, maiden?" Ottar asked her.

Ottar thought for a while, and he came up with a plan whereby he might get Syritha to look at him.

"It is good that you have come here now," he told her. "I am getting married, and as you are here, I would like you to come to the wedding."

And so they held a wedding feast, but Syritha did not look up, so she did not see that the whole thing was a sham.

Then Ottar said: "Syritha, my bride and I are now going to the bridal bed. Will you walk ahead of us and carry a torch to light the way?"

Ottar gave her the torch. It had burned very low, so the flames came closer and closer to her hand. But the determination that burned in that girl's mind was hotter and fiercer than the flames that licked her skin.

After a while, Ottar said to her: "Will you not look at the flames that are burning your hand?"

And Syritha finally looked up. She saw Ottar, and she saw that there was no wedding. At that, the two of them went to the bridal bed together, and she became his wife.

* * *

For notes, see page 160

FRODE's BRIDAL QUEST for HANUNDE

Frode became king when he was still very young. His father had died, and Frode was brought up in the care of two brothers called Westmar and Koll. So these two were Frode's fosterfathers, and they had a good deal of influence over the young king. They also had many sons themselves. But Westmar and Koll and their families abused their position of power terribly, and everyone in the country was afraid of them.

As Frode grew a little older, his men said to him: "Will you not get married this year?"

But Frode was not keen, and he tried to put them off. "I am still very young," he said.

Still they urged him to marry, so Frode went to Westmar and Koll, who were his advisors, and he said to them: "Tell me, do you know of any girl who I might marry, as I have not met anyone?"

"There is one girl," they said. "She is called Hanunde, and she is the daughter of the King of Hunaland. I don't suppose any other girl would be a better choice than her."

But Frode seemed unconvinced by this. He said: "My father often told me that it was better to form the closest alliances with those close to home, and that friendships over long distances were more easily broken."

Westmar's wife was called Gotwara. She was a clever woman with a sharp tongue, and she knew well how to use words to achieve what she wanted. Although she could not use a weapon, she could easily beat any man in an argument using her quick wit. Some she would drown in a flood of well-chosen insults. Others she would lead round and round with clever questions and stubborn answers until they were

all entangled. She could use her words to make peace and form friendships, but she could also use them to spread discord and escalate petty
disagreements, whichever she chose.

When Frode's fostermother heard that he was resisting the advice
he had been given, she decided that she needed to persuade Frode to
listen to what her husband had said. So Gotwara went to see Frode,
and she spoke this verse:

> Weddings belong to the young,
> Old men wait for the grave.

> Youth walks the ways of hope and good fortune,
> Old age slips helplessly down towards death.

> Hope belongs with the young,
> For the old there is hopeless decline.

> All men are doomed to grow old,
> None of us can halt the march of age.

Frode said: "Yes I see you are right. I will propose to this Hunnish
king's daughter. But I need your help. Will you organise the proposal
for me?"

Gotwara said: "I am now an old woman. It would not be easy for
me to do this for you."

But Frode saw that she was refusing only because she wanted pay-
ment from him. So he brought out a beautiful gold necklace. It was
very heavy, and it was decorated with fine patterns and figures of old
kings. "If you do this for me, I will give you this necklace," Frode said
to her. And so it was settled.

So Westmar and Koll and Gotwara and all their sons all set off to
Hunaland on Frode's behalf. When they reached the King of Hunaland, they were well received. They enjoyed the king's hospitality and
feasted in his hall for three days without revealing the reason they had
come.

Before they brought up the matter of the marriage proposal, Westmar wanted to see whether or not the king's daughter would look
favourably on Frode without asking her directly. He thought that he

could gauge her interest though hints and friendly banter, and if for any reason she was against the idea of marrying Frode, he could pretend that he had been joking. So on the third day, when everyone had been drinking hard, he went to speak to her. "What do you think about Frode?" he said.

"I have heard about Frode," she said. "But I am not impressed and not interested in him. What great deeds has he done in his life? What honour or glory has he won? I have not heard of any way that Frode could impress high-born maidens. It seems he is more content to sit at home and do nothing. It hardly matters to me whether Frode is good-looking or not. For honour comes from noble acts and great deeds, and nothing else matters."

When Westmar heard this, he feared the task might be a little more difficult than he had first thought. So he went straight to his wife, as he was sure she could do something to change the maiden's mind.

Then Gotwara went to talk to the king's daughter about Frode, but before she started to speak, she poured a love potion into Hanunde's drink.

"Did you know that Frode is a very good wrestler?" Gotwara said. "He is also an excellent swimmer. Did you know that he can use his left hand just as well as his right?"

And under the influence of the potion, Hanunde started to think that there might be something interesting about Frode after all. The more Gotwara spoke, the more Hanunde started to want and desire Frode.

When this was done, Gotwara told her husband to go and speak to the king. "Tell him why we have come here, and if he chooses to refuse our proposal you must challenge him to fight," she said.

So Westmar and Koll went in to the king, and they took their sons with them, all armed.

"We have come from Frode with a proposal of marriage for your daughter," Westmar said. "It would be better for you to accept this proposal as the alternative is that we challenge you to fight. And know this: we hoped to win honour by coming here, and we would rather meet a noble death than fail in our mission."

The king was not pleased to hear this. "It is not right that low-born men should challenge a king," he said. "Men of different ranks should not fight as equals."

But Westmar raised his sword over the king's head. "We will get something from you," he said. "Either you will give us the maiden we came here for, or you must fight."

The king was ashamed and embarrassed. He did not want to give his daughter to these men, but neither did he want to fight. Looking for a way out, he said: "I have said that my daughter should decide herself who she should marry. So you should go and speak to her about Frode."

When he heard this, Westmar was pleased. He knew how easily women can change their minds, and he thought it would be an easier task to persuade Hanunde to do what he wanted and come back to Frode with them.

So Frode's messengers all went to see the maiden to ask her what she thought about the matter, and her father went with them to hear what she said.

But Hanunde was still under the influence of the love potion that she had drunk. She said this: "Although Frode has achieved nothing in his life, he shows great promise. His father was a great warrior who did many great deeds and won glory and honour. It is only natural that the son of such a man should also go on to achieve great things in time. So I would be very happy to go away with you to marry Frode."

When the King of Hunaland heard his daughter say these things, he was amazed. He knew that he had been outwitted somehow. But as he had allowed his daughter to choose her own husband, he could not go back on that, and so he gave his daughter to Frode. "But I will travel with you," he said. "For there is no-one better to give a daughter away in marriage than the girl's own father."

So they all returned together to Frode: Westmar and Koll and Gotwara and their sons, and the King of Hunaland and Hanunde. The guests were well received. Frode was very pleased to see Hanunde when he met her, and he welcomed her warmly. He also treated her father with great honour, and gave him many gifts of gold and silver. And so Frode and Hanunde were married, and then her father returned to Hunaland.

* * *

For notes, see page 162

ERIK and FRODE

Frode and Hanunde were married, and they lived together in peace for some time. But things were not so peaceful for the people who lived in that country, and that was all down to Westmar and Koll and their families. These two men had fostered Frode, and they still held positions of great power in the country.

Westmar's wife was called Gotwara, and she had borne him twelve sons. Three of them were triplets, and these three were all called Grep. Westmar's brother Koll also had three sons. All fifteen of these young men were fierce warriors. They were brave and fearless, and they loved to fight. But it was peacetime, and there were no wars for them to fight in. And so instead of attacking their enemies, they turned their attention on attacking their own countrymen.

They did many terrible things, and they were not punished for any of it. And when they saw that they had no need to fear any punishment, the things they did grew worse and worse.

They laid goatskins on the ground and pulled them out from under men's feet when they stepped on them so that they fell over. They strung other men up on ropes, and tormented them as they hung helpless in the air. They burned the hair off others, from all over their bodies. Others they beat with bones, and they made others drink until they were dead.

They also held orgies and raped many women. They would go into other men's houses and rape their wives and daughters, whichever they wanted. No woman in the country was safe from them. Rape became commonplace, and everyone in the whole country grew afraid.

They insisted that anyone who wanted to speak to the king should bring a gift, and that anyone who came to see the king without bringing anything would be hanged. They insisted that before any wedding could take place, a special tax must be paid. They also insisted that no maiden was allowed to marry until she had been raped.

Not even Frode's own sister was safe from those men. This girl was called Gunwara the fair because of her great beauty. One of the brothers called Grep decided that he wanted to have her, so she had to flee to a heavily guarded house, and she stayed there and didn't come out. Grep wanted to punish Gunwara for refusing him, so he went to speak to Frode.

"It is time Gunwara got married," he said. "And there are many men who want to marry her. You should call them all here for a feast, then I will speak to them and find out which one would be the best match for her."

So Frode called all the men who wanted to marry Gunwara, and they all came to the feast. But when Grep went to them he hardly spoke at all. Instead, he cut off all their heads. Then he left all the heads in the hall where Gunwara was so that she would find them.

Even this went unpunished, and still they didn't stop. Grep slept with Frode's wife, Hanunde. Grep tried to keep it a secret, and he punished anyone that mentioned it. But the rumours quickly spread, and soon everyone in the country knew what had happened.

So things were not good in Denmark.

* * *

The King of Norway at that time was called Gotar. He heard about everything that was happening in Denmark, and he decided that he might use the situation to his advantage.

Gotar said: "The Danes must hate their king very much as he allows them to live in this state of lawlessness, and they are afraid every day. If I was to attack and overthrow Frode, I would surely be welcomed by those people."

There were two brothers there with the king who heard what he said. They were called Erik and Roller, and they were both sons of the great hero Ragnar by different mothers.

Erik said: "Things might not go as smoothly as you expect if you attack Denmark. It often happens that those who try to take what is not theirs lose what they already have. It is a strong bird that is able to pull something from the claws of another bird while still keeping a grip on what it was holding itself.

"You may find that if you go to Denmark the people will unite to oppose you, for people will always prefer to be ruled by their own countryman than by a foreigner. We have often seen pigs arguing among themselves, but when a wolf approaches the sty they forget their disagreements.

"It would be better for you to send other men to Denmark to assess the situation. Let others help you just as the tongs help the smith. By using the right tools he is able to stop his fingers getting burnt."

When Gotar heard what Erik had to say, he was very impressed by his argument, so he gave him the name well-spoken.

Gotar decided to send a fleet to Denmark under the leadership of a man called Hrafn. The task of defending Denmark's seaways had been given to a man called Odd, who was a kinsman of Frode. This Odd was skilled in magic, and some say that he was a god. He could travel across the water without using a boat, and he could also command the weather. He could summon storm winds or rain clouds or calm weather, whatever he wanted. In this way he could make the sea itself fight on his side and help him destroy his enemies. So Odd was greatly feared by vikings and other seafarers, but he was held in high regard by farmers.

Hrafn came upon Odd's fleet somewhere off the coast of Denmark. Odd's men all drew their swords at once, and the light that came from those blades was so bright that the Norwegians could not look towards it. They turned their faces away. And so it was easy for Odd's men to approach them and cut them down. Many of Hrafn's men were slain, and the survivors fled back to Norway.

When word reached Gotar about what had happened, he started to think that it would not be as easy to attack Denmark as he had hoped. But Gotar also heard that Frode was supported by a very small number of powerful men.

"If there are so few of them it must surely be possible to defeat them and take Denmark that way," the king said.

Roller heard this, and he said to the king: "I will travel to Denmark and to get close to Frode."

When Erik heard what his brother was planning, he was not pleased. He said: "You are a strong man, and you may succeed in what you are planning to do. But that does not mean that it is a good idea."

But Roller would not be dissuaded. "I am sure I will win honour and glory by this," he said.

Erik said: "If you are so set in your mind that you will go to Denmark, then I will go with you, even though I would prefer it if we both stayed here."

* * *

Before Erik and Roller set off on their mission, they went to visit their father Ragnar and his wife Kraka. They went out with Ragnar and counted his cattle with him. Then he took them to the forest, and he showed them where he had buried treasure underground. "You can take whatever you want," he said to them.

Then they returned to the house. They saw smoke coming from the chimney, and they knew that Kraka must be preparing food. Kraka was Roller's mother and Erik's stepmother. Erik looked through a gap in the wall of the house, and he saw what was happening inside. There were three snakes hanging from the roof above the cooking pot. Two were black and one was white. They were all hanging by cords tied around their bellies, and the white snake was hung a little higher. The jaws of all three snakes were gaping wide open, and venom was dripping from their mouths into the food. Erik thought that it was probably magic, but he kept quiet about what he had seen because he didn't want to accuse Kraka of witchcraft.

When the food was ready, they all sat down at the table. Kraka put down a plate of food with white flecks in front of Erik and a plate of food with dark flecks in front of Roller. The food had taken on different colours depending on which of the snakes had left its venom in that part of the food. Erik tasted his food at once, and when he found that he didn't feel the strengthening effect that he was hoping for, he quickly swapped Roller's plate with his own.

"Things often get blown about when there is a storm at sea," he said, making a joke of it.

And so Erik ate the black food with the stronger venom, and Roller ate the white food that his mother had meant for Erik. Erik felt the benefit at once. He felt that he was stronger in his body. But also his mind grew quicker and more alert. His powers of speech and persuasion increased, and he gained a great deal of knowledge. Also he found that he could understand the language of all animals, no matter what brutish sounds they made.

When Kraka saw that the food she had prepared for her own son had been eaten by her stepson, she was annoyed that her scheme had not worked as she had planned. She said to Erik: "Be sure that you look after Roller well on this journey."

And Erik said: "I always look after my brother because it is in my nature to do it."

Kraka also said: "If either of you are ever in great danger and you fear for your lives, call out my name and I will help you."

She was able to say this because she was close to the gods.

* * *

So Erik and Roller sailed away with a fleet. When they came close to Denmark, they met Odd's ships. Erik chose two of his men who could speak the Danish language well.

"Take off your clothes," he said to them, "and swim over to where Odd is. Tell him that you are Danish men, and that I captured you and treated you badly, and that you have now escaped. He will probably be sympathetic if he thinks I took your clothes away. Try to find out his plans and then come back and tell me."

So the men did what Erik asked them. They were able to find out Odd's plans, and they returned to Erik and told him what they had heard.

"Odd has filled his ships with a lot of stones," they said. "He plans to wait until dawn, then he plans to attack us by throwing these stones when we are all still half-asleep."

Erik was particularly pleased when he heard that the enemy ships were filled with stones. That night, he took a little boat, and he rowed alone over to where Odd's ships were. He was as quiet as he could be so that he would not be seen by any of Odd's men who were keeping

watch. He bored holes in the side of one of the ships below the water-line, and then he moved onto the next one. Soon all Odd's ships were filling with water. And because those ships were filled with heavy stones, they all quickly started to sink.

Odd saw what was happening, and he tried to bail out the water using buckets. But while he was doing it, Erik's own ships approached. The Norwegians attacked, and although the Danes tried to fight, their sinking ships were useless. The waves and water fought on Erik's side. Erik's men hardly needed to strike a blow themselves as their enemies sank into the sea. Odd died with all his men, and no-one on the Danish side lived to tell the tale of that massacre.

* * *

Erik continued to sail south through Danish waters. His men had grown hungry, so they landed on an island to see whether they could find any food. There were herds of cattle there, close to the shore. The men rounded up a great number of these cattle and killed them all. Then they skinned the carcases and loaded them onto the ships.

"We should continue on our way," said Erik. So they didn't wait to be discovered, but set sail at once.

But it was not long before the men who owned the cattle found out what had happened. They set off in pursuit of Erik with several ships. When he saw the ships chasing them, Erik said this: "We should tie ropes to the carcases with floating markers, and then throw them all overboard." So that is what they did.

Soon the men who owned the cattle caught up with them, but as they drew alongside and started to shout about the cattle, Erik called out across the water to them: "We don't have your cattle. You are welcome to come onboard and search our ships, but you will not find them."

So the men came onboard as Erik had said, but they found nothing. And as it is difficult to hide a lot of cattle carcases onboard a ship, they decided that it must have been someone else who had taken their cattle. And so they left them.

When those men had gone, Erik returned to the place where the markers were floating on the sea. His men got hold of the ropes and pulled the carcases up from where they had been resting on the sea bed.

When all the carcases were back in the ships they continued on their way.

* * *

Erik's ships reached Zealand, and they landed there so that they could continue on their way to Frode's house over land. Erik was the first to step onto the sand. As he did so, he slipped and fell. But he stood up quickly, and said: "From a bad beginning, things can only get better."

The next one of Frode's men they met was Grep. Grep had heard a rumour that the one who had killed Odd and all his warriors was a well-spoken man. Grep fancied his own skills in arguing, and he thought that he would enjoy beating this man in an argument. Grep did have certain skills, but he was more rude and stubborn than well-spoken. When Grep heard that Erik's fleet had been sighted at a certain harbour, he hurried to that place at once.

As soon as Grep arrived at the place where Erik was, he began to bombard Erik with his argumentative talk.
Grep said:

> Fool, who are you? What's your idle errand?
> Where have you come from, or where are you going?
> Which way are you walking, or what do you want here?
> Who is your father, or what is your line?
>
> They are often stronger, who stay at home,
> The protection of kings, brings prosperity.
> Few praise the deeds, of dishonest men,
> The acts of the enemy, are often hated.

Erik said:

> Ragnar is my father, to some I'm well-spoken,
> I have only ever loved great deeds.
>
> Far I have wandered, in the world so wide,
> Seeking wisdom, and watching the ways of men.
> A fool never knows, the failings of his mind,
> He only follows his urges.

> Lying words, divide the land,
> Just as oars, cleave the ocean.
> Hot air, spreads heartache at home,
> Just as storm winds, stir the sea.

Grep said:

> It is hard to argue, with a babbling halfwit,
> Who speaks a lot, but says little.

Erik said:

> Careless talk, spoken in haste,
> Often returns, to haunt the speaker.
> Words uttered, without understanding,
> Often bring suffering, to the sayer.

> As soon as we see, the ears of a wolf,
> We know that the beast is near.
> Few pay heed, to a false-hearted man,
> Once they have heard, rumours of his treachery.

Grep said:

> Shameless boy,
> Owl flying far from the path,
> Night-owl lost in the light!

> You will soon be sorry, for your reckless speech.
> You will pay with your life, for your witless words.
> Your bloodless body, will be food for the birds,
> Your corpse will be for crows, and greedy beasts.

Erik said:

> The forecasts of a fool, and the wishes of a wicked man,
> Are often found to be unfulfilled.

> One who undermines his master, with immoral schemes,
> Endangers himself, and also his allies.
> A man who fosters a wolf, is feeding a fiend,
> Bringing harm to his own hearth.

Grep said:

> I did not seduce the queen, as you have said,
> I was the defender, of her tender form.
> She brought me good fortune, when I found her favour.

Erik said:

> A man is happiest, when his conscience is clear,
> Your back is bent by guilt.
> A man is reckless, when he relies on his servants,
> A low-born man, may betray his lord.

When he heard this, Grep could think of no answer, and he knew that he had been outwitted. So he leapt onto his horse and rode back to Frode's hall as fast as he could.

* * *

Before too long, Erik and his men also drew near Frode's hall, and Erik realised that he ought to give the king a gift. Now it was midwinter. The air was very cold, and there were fires in every hearth. There was snow on the ground, and all the lakes had frozen. Erik picked up a glistening piece of ice, and he wrapped it in his cloak so that it would not melt when they went inside. Then he went into Frode's house.

As he entered the hall, he stepped onto a goatskin rug that the brothers had laid on the floor. One of those brothers then pulled the rug out from under Erik's feet so that he fell backwards. But his brother Roller was standing behind him, and he caught him so Erik didn't fall onto the floor. The brothers were sitting around the fire, and they howled like wild beasts when they saw Erik tumble. But Erik said: "A man will not fall far when he has a good man behind him."

Then Frode's stepfather Koll spoke to Erik: "If you have come here to see the king then you will have brought him a gift."

Erik said: "I have heard that that is your custom. I have brought this precious stone as a gift for the king." He unwrapped the piece of ice from his cloak and offered it to Koll. But instead of putting it in Koll's hands, Erik dropped the ice into the fire. Everyone who saw this thought that it was Koll who had carelessly dropped the king's gift. They knew that it must be a valuable thing as they could see it glistening and sparkling where it lay in the flames. And then it was gone.

Then Erik said to Frode: "This man has destroyed the gift that I brought here to give to you. If a man who fails to give a gift to the king is to be punished by death, it is right that you should punish him."

And so it was that Koll was hanged.

* * *

Then Frode said to Erik: "Tell me, you who speaks so proudly and talks so loudly, where have you come from, or how did you come here?"

Then Erik said this riddle: "I came from Rennesay, and I came to a stone."

Frode said: "And where did you go then?"

Erik said: "I left a stone and came to a stone. Then I left a stone and passed a stone, and then I came to a stone."

Frode said: "It seems the stones lay thick on the ground where you were."

Erik said: "Yes, but the sand lay thicker."

Frode said: "And where did you go then?"

Erik said: "I left a stone, and then as my ship went on I came to a dolphin."

Frode said: "At last, something new, though rocks and dolphins are both seen in the sea."

Erik said: "Then I saw another dolphin."

Frode said: "Sometimes dolphins swim together in the sea. But where did you go then?"

Erik said: "I went from there and came to a fallen tree. Then I came to a log. I left the log and came to a log."

Frode said: "It seems there were many trees where you were."

Erik said: "And yet there are many more trees in the forest."

Frode said: "And where did you go then?"

Erik said: "I saw many fallen trees, and while I was there, I saw wolves that feast on the bodies of dead men licking the point of a spear. And a saw a spearhead fall from the king's shaft."

Frode said: "Now you have lost me with your riddling. I cannot think what you are trying to say."

Erik said: "If you didn't understand me then I have beaten you with my riddles. I was telling you that I had killed your kinsman Odd at sea on my way here. When I said spearhead, I meant Odd."

Hanunde congratulated Erik on his skill in speaking, and Frode gave Erik a ring from his own arm as a gift.

Then Frode said: "But tell me what you said to Grep when he came to argue with you. It would take something extraordinary to beat that man in an argument."

Erik said: "I simply spoke to him about a certain subject. He was so ashamed that he could not defend himself. He could not argue any more, but had to admit that it was true, and declare himself beaten. We were speaking about the fact that he had been sleeping with your wife."

For a moment Frode didn't know what to say. Then he turned to Hanunde. "Is this true?" he asked her. Hanunde cried out and blushed and looked at the ground. And everyone saw that the story was true.

Then Grep leapt up from where he was sitting by the fire. He rushed at Erik with a spear. But Roller came to his brother's aid. He saw Grep coming, and he drew his sword and cut him down.

When Grep's brothers saw this, they all leapt to their feet and swore they would have revenge.

Erik said: "An act of self-defence is not the same as an unprovoked attack, and a man should not suffer the consequences of deeds that are justly done."

The brothers would not sit down. "Either you will come with ten warriors and fight us, or we will rout your whole fleet," they said.

Erik said: "I see you are determined to fight. So I will do it." Then he turned to the king. "But I ask you for these things. First, I ask for a delay of three days so that I might get ready. Second, I ask that the fight should take place on the frozen surface of the sea, as I am not used to fighting on land. Third, I ask for the hide of a freshly slain ox."

Frode agreed to all these things. "Let the one who fell on a hide have a hide," he said, taunting Erik about his earlier fall.

There was also the question of a punishment for Hanunde.

"What do you think a right punishment for this would be?" Frode asked his wife. Hanunde hesitated. She didn't know what to say. But she begged Frode for forgiveness for her mistake, and the king forgave her.

***

Evening came, and it was time to eat. So everyone gathered in the hall.

Erik said to Frode: "In Gotar's hall, it is usual for guests to sit next to the king in the seats of honour."

Frode didn't want to be seen to be treating his guests worse than the King of Norway, so he let Erik and his men sit in the places where Grep and his brothers usually sat.

The servants brought out plates of fine food for them all to eat. But Erik hardly ate anything. He pulled the food to pieces, tasted a little piece, and then sent the rest back. So the servants brought out more plates of food, and he did the same thing again.

When Frode saw this, he said: "Is it common in Gotar's hall that good food is sent back as though it was scraps, and the best dishes are wasted as though they were leftovers?"

Erik said: "Gotar does not behave in such a rude manner, and there is always good order in his hall."

Frode said: "It seems you have learned little from your lord. A man who goes against his elders shows himself to be a fool."

Erik said: "A wise man must be taught by a wiser man, for knowledge grows greater through learning."

Frode said: "You talk a lot, but what lesson will you teach me?"

Erik said: "It is better to be surrounded by a few good men than by many traitors."

Frode said: "And will you be more loyal to me than the others?"

Erik said: "You still have much to learn." Then he said: "In Gotar's hall it is usual for drink to be served together with the food. Men are usually happier when they have something to drink."

Frode said: "I have never met a more shameless beggar of food and drink."

Erik said: "Few people listen to silent men, and their wishes are seldom granted."

So Frode called his sister Gunwara over and told her to serve drink to Erik. Gunwara filled a cup with wine. That cup was made of gold, all decorated with fine patterns, and it was very beautiful. When Gunwara came to Erik, he took hold of her hand, the one that was holding the cup.

And Erik said to Frode: "This is truly a beautiful thing that you have sent to me. I wonder whether you might give it to me as a gift."

Frode was tired of Erik's chatter. "Yes, you can keep it," he said.

So Erik pulled Gunwara close to him and sat her on his knee.

When Frode saw this, he said: "No you fool, I was talking about the cup, not my sister. You must know that I thought you were asking about the cup."

Erik said: "Well if you don't want me to have the whole thing, maybe I could keep just a little bit." And he made as though he was about to cut off Gunwara's hand with his sword.

Frode saw that he would not beat Erik in any argument, so he gave in and let him have the girl.

* * *

The time chosen for the fight came around. Erik had spent his time preparing for this battle by making special sandals from the oxhide. He smeared the soles of these sandals with a mixture of tar and sand so that whoever was wearing them would not slip on the ice, but could stand surefooted.

So the sons of Westmar and Koll went out onto the frozen sea, and Erik and his men with them. Frode's men could hardly stand up. They struggled to balance as they fought. They slipped and slid on the ice, and they were unsteady on their feet and fell often. But Erik's men had no problem. They were wearing the special sandals that gripped the ice well, and they slew all those brothers.

* * *

The next one of Frode's advisors to challenge Erik was Gotwara, Westmar's wife. This woman was very clever, and she understood well how she could get whatever she wanted through the power of her words. She had no doubt that she would be able to outwit any man in an argument, even Erik who was called the well-spoken.

"I will challenge you to a battle of words," she said to Erik. "If you win, you will get this necklace." She brought out a gold necklace.

It was very heavy, and it was decorated with fine patterns and figures of old kings. Few necklaces were finer than this one. "But if I beat you then you will pay with your life. Do you accept the challenge?"

And so Erik argued with Gotwara. She was humiliated, and so she lost the necklace.

* * *

Westmar had seen his brother hanged, his sons slain, and his wife humiliated, and he was determined to kill Erik. So he challenged him to a rope contest. This was a test of physical strength ? Westmar saw that he would not beat Erik any other way. The two men had to hold onto a loop of rope, and they would both try to wrest it out of the other's hands. The loser would pay with his life.

Erik accepted the challenge, and so they both grasped the rope. It was not long before Erik tugged the rope so hard that Westmar had to let go. The old man was beaten. Erik crushed Westmar's neck with his foot and broke his back. So instead of revenge, Westmar got death, and his name was added to the list of men that Erik had destroyed.

* * *

When Frode saw what was happening, he grew very angry and also afraid, and he decided that he must kill Erik himself. So he took a knife and flung it at Erik. But Gunwara saw what her brother was doing and called out to warn Erik. He leapt out of the way, and the knife embedded itself in the wall of the hall.

Erik said: "Thank-you for this knife. You are a good king who gives such precious gifts to his friends. It is usually better for gifts to be placed in the hands rather than thrown. I would like this knife all the more if you also gave me a sheath to go with the blade."

Frode was astonished by Erik's self-control. He took the sheath from his belt and handed it to Erik. He couldn't think of anything else he could do.

* * *

That night, Gunwara woke Erik as he lay asleep. She said this: "It would be better if we left at once. I don't know what my brother has planned, but I fear things could quickly get worse for us if we stay here."

So Erik gathered all his men, and they made their way back to their ships on the shore. But first, Erik and Gunwara went to Frode's ships and cut the planks so that they would surely sink out at sea. They also disguised what they had done so that it would not be seen. Then they returned to their own ships and set sail.

When Frode saw that Erik had left, he rushed to his ships on the shore with whatever men he could find to act as crew, and he set off in pursuit at once. But it was not long before Frode's ships had let in so much water that they began to sink and break up. Frode was in the water, and he could hardly swim as he was weighed down by the heavy armour he was wearing. But Erik and Roller leapt into the sea, and they swam over to where Frode was flailing helplessly in the water. Three times Frode sank down into the waves, and three times Erik and Roller pulled him up again. They pulled him back to their own ship and helped him onboard. They got the king's wet gear off him, and dressed him in dry clothes. Frode was shivering and breathless, and could do nothing except cough up seawater for a long time. But after a while, he started to talk.

"What are you doing?" said Frode. "Will you not even let me die? You have taken everything I have from me. You have killed my stepfathers and their families, you have taken my sister, you have taken my treasure, I have lost my wife, but worst of all I have no honour left. I have been defeated and humiliated in every way by a common man. I have nothing left to live for, and now you will not leave me to die as I want but put me in your debt by saving my life. You must kill me now, or I will kill myself."

Erik said: "Turn your mind away from these thoughts. The truth is that often we must go through troubles to find better times. You are surely strong enough to recover from all this and to go on and be thought of as a great man.

"When we came to you, you were not free. In fact we came here to help you. Look, I will give you back what I have taken from you. Here are your treasures and other things. If you think the way your sister was given to me was improper, then let her marry the man you choose yourself. We have not yet slept together.

"Also, I want to serve you. I hope that you accept my service. You have lost none of your freedom and none of your power. I will obey you."

And so Erik was able to persuade Frode that things were not so bad after all, and they all returned to Frode's hall. Frode agreed again to give his sister in marriage to Erik, and he also put a number of men under his command.

The matter of Hanunde still had to be settled. Gotwara was hung for her part in the deception, and Frode said that he would send Hanunde back to her father.

But Erik said: "Would it not be better if she was to stay here and marry my brother?" and Frode agreed.

And so Erik married Gunwara, and Roller married Hanunde. The two weddings were held on the same day, and they were all very happy. But Frode was left without a wife.

* * *

For notes, see page 164

FRODE's BRIDAL QUEST for ALFHILD

Erik said to Frode: "So now you are without a wife, you will need to marry again."

Frode said: "I don't know of any girl who I might marry."

Erik said: "I know of a maiden. She is called Alfhild, and she is the daughter of King Gotar of Norway. I don't suppose any other girl would be better for you than her."

Frode said: "Will you go to Norway then, to arrange the proposal for me?"

And Erik said: "I will do it."

And so it was that Erik and his brother Roller sailed back home to Norway. They both took their wives with them, Gunwara and Hanunde, as neither of them could bear to be parted from their husbands. When they reached Norway, they went at once to visit Kraka. They found that their father had died, and that Kraka had remarried. Her new husband was called Brak. So they went to the place in the forest where their father had told them that he had buried his treasure. They dug up the gold and took it back their ship, and Kraka and Brak went with them.

Word reached Gotar that Erik had returned to Norway, and he grew apprehensive. Gotar thought to himself: "Erik has been away in Denmark for some time. He has grown more powerful and influential, and I am sure he has lost none of his way with words. It would be better to make sure Erik is an ally than to wait while he grows strong enough to become a rival."

Gotar heard that Erik was coming to propose marriage to his daughter on behalf of Frode, and he knew that Erik had married Frode's sister. But Gotar's wife had recently died, and Gotar wanted very much to marry Gunwara himself. He thought that if he married Gunwara, there would be an alliance between himself and Frode, and that if he gave his own daughter Alfhild to Erik, there would be an alliance there as well, just as he wanted. "It is inconvenient that Gunwara is married to Erik," Gotar thought. "But I suppose Erik would be happy enough to give her up if he got Alfhild instead."

Word soon reached Erik about what Gotar was planning, and Erik was not pleased by what he heard. He had come to fetch a wife for Frode, not to give up his own wife, who he loved very much. So Erik thought for a while until he had come up with a plan to outwit Gotar and get what he wanted.

First Erik went to speak to his wife. "Do you have any love for Gotar?" he asked her. "I have heard that he hopes to marry you, and everyone knows that it is better for royal girls to marry kings rather than common men."

"Why are you asking this?" Gunwara said. "Tell me you are joking."

"I am not joking," Erik said. "I am very serious."

And then Gunwara burst into tears. "I thought I had married an honest man," she said. "But now I see you would trade me as though I was any thing that belonged to you. When I was a maiden, you loved me very much, but now I am your wife it seems you want to be rid of me."

Then Erik took her into his arms, and he said to her: "I am not going to give you to anyone. Gotar will not have you. Death is the only thing that will take me away from you. I needed to be sure that you were loyal to me. I have a plan so that we can come out of here with what we came for, but I need your help."

"I will do whatever you advise," Gunwara said. And so Erik explained his plan to her.

Then Erik went to speak to his men. He said: "I have heard that Gotar means to make it difficult for us to carry out our mission. If we are to succeed in doing what we came here to do, we must go against him. But fortune rarely favours those who attack a man with no reason. So we will turn tail and flee from here, and see whether Gotar gives chase and tries to attack us first."

So they turned the ship around and started to sail away. When Gotar saw this, he called out to his men, and rushed down to his own ship at once. Gotar sailed hard after Erik, and was gaining on him. But then Erik quickly turned his ship around to face Gotar.

Gotar called out across the water: "Who is sailing this ship?"

Erik replied: "My name is Erik."

Gotar said: "Are you the same Erik that is able to outwit all other men by the power of his speech?"

Erik said: "I have been called well-spoken before."

And so the two of them agreed to go to the shore and talk.

Erik said: "I have come here on Frode's behalf to propose marriage to your daughter."

Gotar said: "I would rather offer you my daughter to you to marry yourself, while I married Frode's sister. That way the alliance would be formed between Frode and myself through my marriage to Gunwara. But also you would be rewarded for your work as a messenger. I would be pleased to have you for my son-in-law."

Erik said: "You show great wisdom in this proposal, and the gods themselves could not make a kinder offer. But we should ask Gunwara what she has to say about this arrangement." And so they went over to speak to Gunwara.

"I would be happy to marry you, Gotar," she said. "But I ask that the wedding between Erik and Alfhild should happen first. That way when I am married to you I will not feel bad for deserting my former husband. Also, the two wedding feasts should be held in separate rooms in your hall. That way my eyes would not be tempted to look at my former husband during the feast. They would only look at you, Gotar."

Gotar thought that this sounded reasonable, so he agreed to what Gunwara said.

Then they all went together to Gotar's hall to prepare for the two weddings. Erik's stepmother Kraka was with them. She kept her head completely covered by her cloak all the time. Whenever any of Gotar's men asked who it was, she said that she was Gunwara's sister, and that she had to keep her head covered to protect her eyes. They all believed her because there was no doubt that she was a woman.

Erik also spoke to Brak. "Wait in secret a little way away from the hall with your fiercest warriors," he said. "If I need your help I will give you a signal."

Things happened just as Erik had planned. The two wedding feasts were to be held in Gotar's hall, but a dividing wall was built between the two rooms to keep the feasts separate, just as Gunwara had asked. Before the feasts started, Erik went there and removed a panel from that dividing wall behind the wall hangings. In that way, it was possible for someone to pass through the wall in secret.

So the feasts began. In one room, Gotar sat beside Gunwara. In the other, Erik sat with Alfhild on one side, and his stepmother Kraka on the other.

As the feast went on, Erik said to Alfhild: "I came here to propose marriage to you on behalf of Frode, but now your father prefers that you marry me. But tell me, what would you prefer to do?"

Alfhild said: "I have no wish to do anything other than what my father wants."

Erik said: "I have often heard it said that it is better for a king's daughter to marry another king, and not to marry a common man. In that way, she would not lose her high rank as a result of the low status of her husband. If you were to marry Frode, you would become Queen of Denmark, and I suppose you would also become very rich, richer than other women."

And so by this talk, Erik was soon able to persuade Alfhild that she should go away with him and marry Frode. Some say that Kraka helped Erik through her witchcraft: she put a love potion into the girl's drink that caused her to fall in love with Frode.

It happened that Gotar decided that he would go from his own feast to visit the other feast in the other room. When Gunwara saw him doing this, she did as Erik had told her, and secretly passed through the hole in the wall. So she also went to the other room where Erik and Alfhild were. But she arrived there ahead of Gotar and sat down next to Erik.

Gotar was amazed when he walked into the other room and saw her there. "What are you doing here, Gunwara," he said. "Or how did you get here?"

"I am not Gunwara," she said to him. "I am Gunwara's sister. I understand that you are mistaken as we look so alike."

Gotar could not believe his eyes. So he returned to his own feast at once. Gunwara was there ahead of him as she passed through the wall again, and was sitting in her own place when Gotar came in.

The king could hardly believe it. It was not just that these two sisters looked similar, they were indistinguishably alike. He could find no difference between them. So again he returned to Erik's room, and again Gunwara got there ahead of him by secretly passing through the wall. It seemed that wherever Gotar looked, he saw Gunwara.

When the feasts were over, Gotar led Erik and Alfhild to the bridal bed, as was the custom, and then he left them. But Erik told Alfhild to sleep apart from him, as she would marry Frode. And he slept with Gunwara as usual.

Meanwhile Gotar lay in bed alone, and he could not sleep. He knew he had been outwitted somehow but he didn't know how. Finally it came to him that there might have been a hole in the dividing wall. So he leapt up and summoned his men. "Go down and check the dividing wall," he told them.

But Erik had already repaired the hole in the wall, and the men could find nothing wrong with it. Gotar was even more bewildered when he heard this. Then he said to his men: "Go to Erik and Alfhild's room in secret and see whether you can find out what is going on. If you find that Erik is sleeping with Gunwara, you should kill him at once."

So the king's men went to that room and hid behind the wall hangings. As they looked out, they could clearly see Erik and Gunwara lying in each other's arms. "We will wait until he is asleep," they whispered to each other.

It wasn't long before Erik gave out a loud snore, and those men were sure that he was asleep. But Erik heard them as they came out from their hiding place and came towards the bed. He looked up and saw the raised swords, and he remembered what his stepmother had told him: that if he was ever in great danger and feared for his life, he should call out her name.

So Erik called out "Kraka!"

And she did not fail to keep her word. A shield that had been hanging above the bed fell down at that moment to cover and protect Erik's body. Then Erik reached for his sword, and was able to cut both feet off the man who was nearest to him. Gunwara picked up a spear and ran it through the other. For although she had the body of a woman, she had the spirit of a man.

"It is time for us to go now," Erik said.

So all Erik's party were roused from their beds and they hurried down to the ship, and Alfhild with them. Brak and his band of warriors took as much of the king's treasure as they could carry down to the ship, and then they all set sail.

When morning came and Gotar saw that they had gone, he started to get ready to give chase at once.

But his advisors said: "It would be better not to act in haste. If he reaches Denmark then you will need more men with you than you have here now. You will not win anything with these few men. It would be better to wait and plan an attack carefully."

But the king did not listen. He set off in pursuit. But before he caught up with Erik, the weather worsened. The king's ships came in to land at a place called Omi, but while they were waiting there for better weather the food supplies ran out, and the men saw that soon they would all die. "It would be better if we were to die fighting than to die a slow death from starvation," the king's men said. So they agreed to fight among themselves. They drew their swords, and soon they were all dead. Gotar fled inland into the high fells with a few men to take their chances there.

Meanwhile, Erik reached home in fair weather, and Alfhild and Frode were married.

* * *

For notes, see page 162

FRODE's PEACE and the END of FRODE

Frode won many victories and conquered many lands, and when all this was done, he ruled over a great empire. But after he had destroyed so much in war, he wanted to bring peace to all men. Frode introduced laws to all the lands that he ruled over to make sure that everyone living there would be protected. Now that there was no danger of attack from abroad, he wanted to make sure that the property of his people would be protected from thieves, and they might live peacefully in their own homes without fear of theft.

As a public test and demonstration of the honesty of the people, Frode hung heavy gold arm rings in prominent places by the sides of main roads in his country. The gold rings were hung up at the cross-roads. They were unguarded, and could easily be reached and taken by anyone. Many men were tempted to take one of the rings, but they were all afraid of Frode and what he would do if he found out that a ring had been taken, and so the rings stayed where they were.

* * *

There was a certain woman who was skilled in magic. She believed that her magic would protect her from whatever punishment Frode would try to give if she stole one of the rings. So she tried to persuade her son to take the ring.

"Frode is almost dead," she told him. "His body is weak and his mind is feeble. You have nothing to fear from him."

But her son was very afraid of Frode. "I will be heavily punished if I take the ring," he said.

"If Frode tries to punish you, he will see a female walrus and its calf, and things will not turn out well for him," the woman replied.

So the son was persuaded that his mother would protect him from whatever punishment Frode would try to give, and he went to the crossroads and took the ring that Frode had put there.

When Frode heard about this, he was very angry. He summoned all his men, and they travelled at once to the house where the woman lived with her sons, meaning to arrest them all. At that time, Frode was old and his body was weak, so he mainly travelled in a carriage.

But when they arrived at the woman's house, there was no-one at home. The woman had heard that Frode was on his way, and she had transformed herself into a walrus, and her sons into walrus calves.

Frode saw the walruses down on the seashore, and he thought it was a great marvel.

"I will get down from this carriage," he said, "and go down to the shore to better look at those animals. You, men, go between the walruses and the sea to stop them returning to the water."

So Frode got down and walked down onto the beach. He came close to where the walruses were so that he might see them better, and then he sat on the ground and watched.

But then the female walrus rushed at Frode and gored him with its tusk so that he died. It was a sad death for such a great king. When Frode's men saw what had happened, they attacked the female walrus and all the calves, and spiked them with their spears until they were all dead.

"It is strange," the men said, "that the bodies of those walruses we have killed look like human corpses with animal heads."

The men knew then that they were dealing with some powerful magic.

* * *

After Frode's death, the noblemen wanted to keep the peace that Frode had brought to all the lands that he ruled over. They didn't want to make it known that Frode had died, as they feared that if word got out, it may lead to fighting and lawlessness.

So they had Frode's body disembowelled and embalmed, and they placed the lifeless corpse on a carriage as though Frode was sitting up. And for three years after Frode's death, they took the body all around his lands. Anyone who saw Frode sitting in the carriage didn't doubt that he was still alive, though he may have been old, infirm, and untalkative. And while those men took Frode's body around on the carriage, the peace prevailed.

But after a while, the body started to decay, and the rot could not be stopped. So a funeral was held, and Frode's body was buried in a barrow on Zealand.

* * *

For notes, see page 162

HADDING and HARDGREP

King Gram had two sons. Hadding he had with Signe, and Guthorm with Groa. These two boys were sent to Sweden by boat to be fostered with two giants called Wagnhofde and Hafle.

While Hadding was still young, he grew tall and strong. He trained hard in fighting methods, as he knew that he would live his life as a warrior.

Wagnhofde had a daughter, who was called Hardgrep. She was very fond of Hadding, and had nursed him when he was very young. But as he grew up, she wanted him to take her into his bed and to make her his wife.

This is what Hardgrep sang to Hadding:

Why do you wander, through life unwed,
And let the years pass you by?
Why do you follow, the call of battle,
Thinking nothing, of a woman's embrace?

You think only of war, long only for slaughter,
You don't see my beauty, don't think about love.

I gave you milk, and was a mother for you,
When you were young and helpless,
Now let your hard heart soften,
And give your love to me.

But Hadding was unconvinced. "It is difficult for a man to embrace such an enormous body as yours," he said. "Also, men and giants are very different in nature. Such a marriage would not work."

So Hardgrep sang on:

> Do not dismiss me, due to my bulk,
> Sometimes I grow, as high as the heavens,
> Sometimes I shrink, to a woman's size,
> My body can change, however I choose.

Still Hadding was unmoved. So Hardgrep sang on:

> Do not fear, the pleasure of my body,
> Share my bed, and share my heart.
>
> Now I grow broad, but now narrow,
> Again and again, I shift my shape.
>
> I can tell you, I have two forms.
> Sometimes my head, soars in the sky,
> My shoulders touch, the tops of the clouds,
> And my eyes are beside, the shining stars.
>
> But then I shrink, to a smaller shape,
> Remould myself, like marvellous wax,
> And you will find me, in human form.
>
> When I am huge, I terrify the fiercest warriors,
> But when I am small, I need the love of a man.

Finally, Hadding agreed to make Hardgrep his wife, and the two of them became lovers.

In the meantime, King Gram had been killed. His two sons reacted differently to the news. Guthorm was happy to make peace with his father's killer. But Hadding swore that he would avenge his father. So Hadding set off to travel to Denmark. But Hardgrep was so much in love with Hadding that she could not bear for the two of them to be parted. So she cut out men's clothes for herself, and she went with him. In that way, she thought that she could be with him through any trouble that he might meet, and that she might help to protect him.

One night as they were travelling, they reached a house as dusk was falling, and they called to ask for shelter for the night. It happened that the man who lived in that house had recently died, and the funeral rites were being held for him.

Hardgrep saw an opportunity here. She thought that she would be able to summon the spirit of the dead man using magic, and ask him certain things about the otherworld. So she carved runes on a piece of bark, and told Hadding to put the bark under the man's tongue. When he did this, the dead man began to speak in a terrible voice:

To the one who dragged me up, I bring death,
A charm I will chant, and a curse I will cast.

The one who called on me, wakening the dead,
Lifting the lifeless, from the lower realm,
Bringing me out again, onto the earth,
She will pay, for her rash actions.

Listen to my song, soon I will sing it,
I will bring you bad news, that you won't want to hear.

When you have gone, and left this house behind,
You will wander on a path, winding through the woods,
Trolls will come for you, out of the trees,
And fearsome giants, will find you in the forest.

And there the one, who brought me back,
Casting me into, this cold–bodied corpse,
To look on the light, of the world again,
Will sorely rue, her recklessness.

To the one who dragged me up, I bring death,
A charm I will chant, and a curse I will cast.

Her innards will be pulled, and her entrails drawn out,
Her limbs will be split, and her legs torn off,
And cruel claws, will crush her life.

You, Hadding, will not be harmed,
You will walk on, alone across the earth.

But the woman who summoned, the sleeping spirit,
She will be punished, for her crime against the ghost,
Soon she will be a ghost herself.

To the one who dragged me up, I bring death,
A charm I have chanted, a curse I have cast.

And things happened just as the dead man had foretold. Hadding and Hardgrep continued on their way, and later they stopped to spend a night in a forest. They made a shelter framed with sticks. But as they rested that night in the shelter, an enormous hand appeared, moving over their heads. When Hadding saw this, he called out to Hardgrep for help. Hardgrep grew at once to an enormous size, and gripped the hand hard while Hadding cut it off at the wrist. It was not blood that flowed out of the wound, but a disgusting slime.

Things did not go well for Hardgrep after that. Many more creatures of the same kind appeared, and her size and powers could not help her against so many. They picked her up and tore her to pieces. And so Hardgrep died, and Hadding lost his lover and his fostermother.

* * *

For notes, see page 166

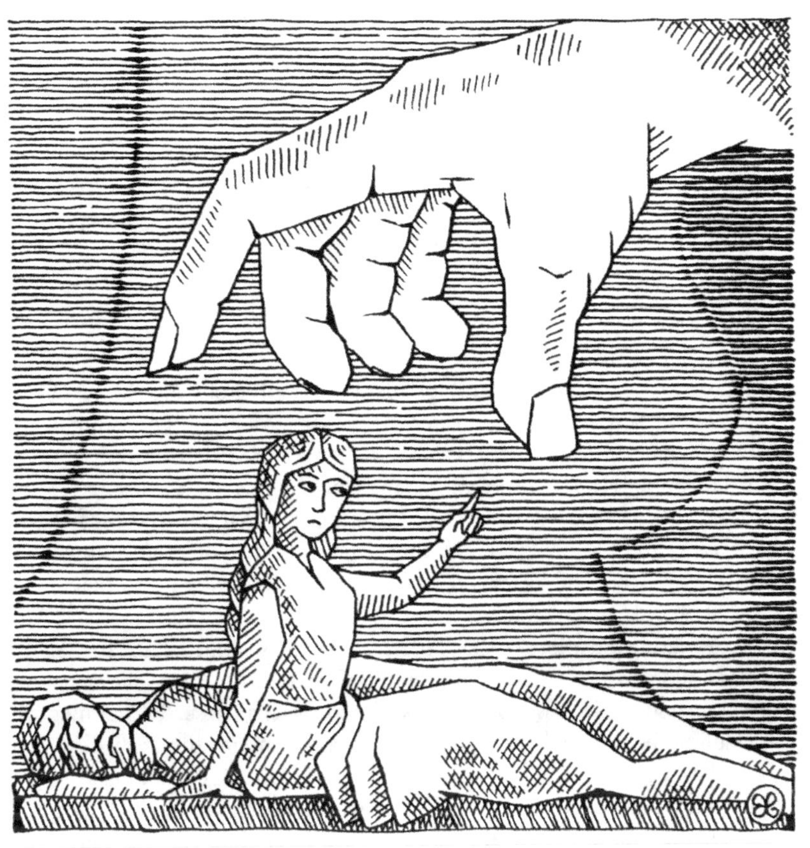

HADDING and RAGNHILD, and HADDING's JOURNEY to the UNDERWORLD

News reached Hadding that Ragnhild, the daughter of King Hakon of the Nitherians, had been promised in marriage to a giant. The thought of this marriage disgusted Hadding, and he was determined to stop it if he could. He thought that a giant would make a very unsuitable husband for a king's daughter. Hadding thought that if he travelled to Norway and fought and killed that same giant, it would be counted as a great deed, and he would win honour and glory by it. So that is what he did.

Hadding did kill the giant, but he was badly wounded in the battle. Ragnhild was grateful for what Hadding had done for her, so she came to him and tended his wounds herself. But this maiden had never met Hadding before, and she was worried that she might forget his face. So she took a ring and hid it inside one of the wounds in Hadding's leg so that when the wound was healed it would leave a mark.

Some time after that, the time came for Ragnhild to choose a husband for herself. All the young men who had come to court her were gathered in the hall. Hadding was there as well, but Ragnhild didn't know which one he was.

Then Ragnhild asked all the young men to show their legs, and she went along the line and felt the legs of each of them carefully. When she got to Hadding, she felt the ring that she had hidden in his leg, and she knew that this was the man who had slain the giant for her sake.

"This is the man I choose," she said.

And so a great feast was held for the wedding. While this was going on, a woman appeared by the hearth. She was carrying a bunch of fresh hemlock in her hand, even though it was the middle of winter.

The woman spoke to Hadding: "Tell me, where do you think I could find these herbs at this time of year?"

But Hadding said: "I don't know, but perhaps that is something you will tell me."

"I will show you," the woman said. Then she wrapped Hadding in her cloak, and she vanished into the ground, taking Hadding with her.

The truth was that the gods of the underworld wanted Hadding to visit their realm before his death.

First, Hadding and the woman passed through a dark and misty cloud. They walked along a well-trodden path that had been worn away by many footsteps. On that path, they passed many rich and well-dressed men.

After a while, they reached a sunny meadow where plants were growing. "This is where I collected the herbs," the woman said.

They walked on and further on, and soon they came to the edge of a wide river, fast flowing and deep. The dark waters rolled and tumbled, and swirled with currents. And there was a bridge that spanned the river. It was the only way across.

After they had crossed the bridge, they came to a place where two mighty armies were fighting. "Who are these men, or why are they fighting?" Hadding asked the woman.

"These are dead men, fallen in battle," she said. "They are doomed always to fight here, reenacting their last battles and the moments of their deaths."

They passed by the fighting men, and then they came to a high wall. The woman tried to jump over the wall, but she could not do it. It was too high. She had brought a cock with her. She wrung the bird's neck so that it was dead, and then she flung it high into the air so that it went over the wall. Then at once both of them heard the cock crow, as it had come back to life.

After that, Hadding returned to his place at the wedding feast.

* * *

Hadding returned to Denmark with his bride. On the way, they were attacked by vikings, but Hadding escaped from them by swift sailing. For even though it was the same wind that blew Hadding's ship and the viking ships, Hadding was able to sail faster.

Hadding and Ragnhild lived together in peace for many years after that. He gave up his life as a viking warrior, and lived with his wife in the countryside far from the sea. He never once took up arms, but held only farmer's tools in his hands. But as the years passed, Hadding began to grow tired of the quiet life. He missed the excitement of his old life, and started to long for war. He sang this song:

> Why should I huddle, hidden in shadows,
> My heart is stifled, by these high hills.
> I long for the swell, of the open sea,
> Where I often sailed before.
>
> The howls of wolves, rise to the heavens,
> The cries of wild beasts, echo through the land.
>
> I would rather go back, to the sea again,
> Sailing a ship, across salty sounds,
> Gathering gold, and other great treasures,
> And winning glory, with a following wind,
> Than remain here, in these unyielding mountains.

But Ragnhild was happy with her life in the countryside. She did not miss the cries of the seabirds, but was much happier walking in the woods. She sang:

> The shrieking of gulls, by the seashore tires me,
> Their endless chatter, keeps me from sleep.
> The screeching birds, wheeling in from the sea,
> Rob me of rest, with their morning racket.
>
> I find no comfort, in the seagulls' cry.
> Their miserable mewing, brings only suffering,
> And a sad promise, of sorrows to come.

It is better to live, safe on the land,
Where food is easily, found on the farm,
Than to be unhappily tossed, 'cross the shifting sea.

* * *

For notes, see page 166

HADDING's DAUGHTER

After Ragnhild had died, she appeared to Hadding in a dream, and she sang this song to him:

> You have fathered, a fearsome monster,
> Raging and ferocious, like a ravenous wolf.
> He will quell the anger, of wild animals.
>
> And you have fathered, a fierce bird,
> Angry as an owl, out in the night,
> But with the sweet song, of a tuneful swan.

When Hadding woke up, he was very troubled, and he went at once to a seer who was skilled in the interpretation of dreams.

This is what the seer said to Hadding: "The wolf means your son, he will win victory over his enemies in battle. The bird is your daughter, she will betray her father."

And things happened just as they had been foretold.

Hadding's daughter was called Ulfhild, and she had married a common man, who was called Guthorm. Perhaps she was unhappy about her husband's low status. Perhaps she would rather have been called a queen than a king's daughter. It seems, though that she did not love her father as a daughter should. She tried to persuade her husband to murder her father, and she sang this song to him:

Unhappy am I, a high-born girl,
Brought down, by an unmatched marriage.
Misery is mine, a noble maiden,
Bound for life, to a lowly commoner.
Luckless lady, daughter of a king,
Whose worthless father, gave her away,
Wedded to a lesser man.

Listen, husband, if you have any honour,
If you deem yourself worthy, of a king's daughter:
Seize the crown, soon from my father,
Take through courage, what should be yours.

Your blood is not noble, so prove that you are brave,
Your lineage is lowly, so show your spirit.
Power that is won, by your own acts,
Is reckoned more worthy, than inherited rights.

There is no shame, in toppling an old man,
Who is already stumbling, into the grave.
If you do not hasten, to take the crown,
Someone else, soon will have it.
Anything that rests, on old age,
Will not last long.

I would rather my husband was king than my father,
I would rather be a queen, than a king's daughter,
I would rather have the king, in my own home,
Than pay him homage, from far away.

And wouldn't you rather, wear the crown,
Than be forced to follow, your wife's father?
I know this is true, it is in our nature:
We all love, ourselves the best.

If there is a will, a way will be found,
For many things are mastered, by the minds of men.

A feast will be held, in the high hall,
Carefully we will prepare, and the king will come,
The road to betrayal, is smoothed by false friendship,
Traps are easiest to hide, from those we hold closest.

Do not hesitate, to strike with your hand,
Let him feel, the steel in his flesh,
And what we both want, will soon be ours.

Guthorm was persuaded by Ulfhild's words. "We will invite your father to come here to our house for a feast," he said. "And it will be done then."

But when Hadding heard that he had been invited to his son-in-law's house, he remembered the words of warning from his dream, and he took an armed guard with him. "Wait here," he said to them when they were close to the house. "And come in only if you hear my signal."

So Hadding went into the house, and he sat down at the table to eat and drink. But Hadding saw a man with a dagger hidden under his cloak, and knew that he must be an assassin, come to kill him. So Hadding blew on his horn. His men heard the signal, and they came into the hall at once and came to the king's aid. The ones who had plotted against the king paid dearly for their lack of loyalty.

* * *

For notes, see page 166

The DEATHS of HUNDING and HADDING

Hadding's death had been prophesied some years earlier. It happened like this. One time, Hadding was sailing northwards past the coast of Norway, on his way to fight against the men of Bjarmeland. He saw an old man standing on the sea shore signalling to him, waving his cloak.

"We should sail in to land to see what that man wants," Hadding said to his men.

"Let us sail on," they said. "We will reach Bjarmeland sooner if we don't stop, and what use will this old man be to us?"

But Hadding insisted that they sailed in to the shore, and so the old man was taken onboard.

When they reached Bjarmeland, the man gave Hadding some advice about fighting. "You should use a wedge formation," he said. "Two men furthest forward, four behind them, eight behind them, and so on. I will stand furthest back with the archers and slingers."

Then the old man took a crossbow from a pouch that was handing around his neck. It seemed small at first, but it grew bigger and bigger. The man fitted ten arrows to the bow, and shot them all at once, over the heads of Hadding's men towards to the men of Bjarmeland.

Things went badly for the men of Bjarmeland in that battle. But when those men saw that their fighting skills were failing them, they turned to magic instead. They summoned rain clouds, and soon the air was drenched with falling rain. But the old man countered this magic with his own. He summoned mist clouds that drove the rain away, and the victory went to Hadding.

Before he left them, the old man said this to Hadding: "You should not fight petty battles, but only those wars where you might win honour. You should not waste your time with small fights close to home, but travel far and wide to win glory. What is more, I see that your death will come not from the might of your enemies, but from your own hand."

* * *

This prophecy was fulfilled, and this is how it happened. Many years later, false news reached King Hunding of Sweden that Hadding was dead. Hunding believed the story, and he was upset to hear it. He decided to hold a funeral feast in Hadding's honour, and he invited all his noblemen. Hunding had a huge jar set in the middle of his hall, and had it filled with ale. At the feast, it was Hunding himself who acted as cup-bearer, and refilled the cups of the noblemen.

But while he was doing this, he slipped and fell into the jar. Hunding drowned in the ale and was dead.

Perhaps this happened to appease the god of death, who was offended that a funeral feast was being held when no-one had died. Or perhaps it happened to appease Hadding, after Hunding had spread false news about his death.

When news of what had happened reached Hadding, he decided that he would repay Hunding for the honour that he had given him. So he called all his people together and he hanged himself in front of them. And that was how Hadding died.

* * *

For notes, see page 166

HARALD, ODIN, and the WEDGE FORMATION

There was once a king called Harald. His birth and death were both foreseen by Odin's oracle. So it was natural that Odin played a significant part in Harald's life.

When Harald was still very young, he went to fight in a battle alongside his father. But things did not go well, and Harald's father was slain. Harald's mother was called Gurid, and she was also at that same battle. She loved her son so much that she could not bear to be parted from him, so she had cut out men's clothes for herself and was fighting alongside the men. Gurid saw that her husband had fallen, and that Harald was bravely fighting alone as his companions had fled, so she went over to where her son was. She lifted him up onto her shoulder, and carried him away from the battlefield and into the woods to safety. But as he was sitting there on his mother's shoulder, an enemy archer shot an arrow that pierced his buttocks. So Gurid's concern for her son brought him more shame than help.

Harald grew up to be very tall and handsome, and also strong. He was also favoured by Odin with this gift: that he could not be wounded by steel. It was also said that the souls of all those who were slain by Harald's sword were promised to Odin.

One time, a Swedish king attacked Denmark, and Harald consulted an oracle to find out how the battle would go. An old man appeared to him. He was very tall, and he was missing one eye. He was also dressed in a hairy cloak. This man was called Odin, and he said this to Harald: "Whenever you fight a battle on land, you should arrange your troops in this way. Divide your troops into three groups. Each of these groups should be in a wedge formation. Two men should stand furthest forward, and behind them the number should increase by two in each row. Behind these should be young men armed with spears, and furthest back should be slingers and archers, who can attack the enemy from some distance away using missiles."

Odin also gave Harald other advice about fighting at sea. Using this advice, Harald was able to defeat the Swedish attack, and he also won many other battles after that.

* * *

There was a certain Ring, who was the son of Harald's sister by a Swedish king. The boy's father died while he was still very young, and so Ring became king when he was hardly old enough to rule alone. Harald arranged guardians and advisors for Ring, and he taught him much about kingship himself. So Harald and Ring were bound by both friendship and blood, and they became great allies.

Many years later, Harald had grown old. His main advisor at this time was a man called Brun. Brun had been fostered with Harald, and so Harald trusted him very much. Ring also trusted Brun, and so the two kings used this man to take secret messages from one to the other.

But one time, Brun was travelling between Harald and Ring when he fell into a river and drowned. When this happened, Odin took on Brun's appearance. He continued to meet with Harald and Ring, and neither of them suspected that it was anyone other than Brun. But Odin had something else in mind. He planned to sow discord between the two kings. And so by whispering in both their ears, he was able to stir up resentment. This was kept secret at first, but it built up until both of them openly declared their hate for the other. It seemed that the only way to solve their disagreement was through war, and so they started to prepare for battle.

Harald had grown old and infirm, and by now he was also blind, but he did not want to die peacefully at home. He preferred to end his life in the same way that he had lived it, so that his death should be consistent with his past deeds. He also thought that his death would be even more glorious if he died with many other men in a great battle, and so he secretly wanted to be beaten by Ring.

The time for the battle came, and huge numbers of men travelled to fight. As they all gathered on the battlefield, Ring spoke to his troops.

He said: "We will wait here until Harald has arranged his troops, and we see him in his chariot beside the standards. I have no doubt that we will win victory over Harald today. An army that follows a blind man into battle is easily defeated. Harald has grown old, and has lost his mind as well as his sight. It is strange that he should think of attacking us here now when he should be thinking about his own grave."

Meanwhile, Harald had instructed Brun to arrange his troops for him, so he got them into a wedge formation. Harald spoke to his men from his chariot, and then the battle began.

When the trumpets sounded and the fighting started, it was as though the sky had fallen down on the earth, and the fields and woods sank into the ground. It was as though the end of the world had come, and heaven and earth were mingling together in turmoil. The clash of steel filled the air with a roar of thunder, the steam of wounds hung above the battlefield like a mist, and daylight was hidden by a hail of spears. Many men fought bravely, and many heroes fell. There were even some warrior women who fought at that battle, cutting champions down.

From his chariot, Harald heard his men cry out in distress, and he turned to Brun, who was driving the chariot.

Harald said: "How does Ring have his troops arranged?"

Brun smiled and said: "He has his men in a wedge formation."

Harald was astonished when he heard this, and he started to panic. He said: "How can this be? That formation was thought up by Odin, and he taught it to no-one but me."

But Brun said nothing, and finally Harald realised that the one driving his chariot was none other than Odin himself. Harald started to beg Odin for help, as he had helped him in the past. But Odin could withhold help just as well as he could give it. Odin pushed Harald out of the chariot onto the ground. As the old man fell, Odin snatched the club out of his hand. Then he turned and smashed the club into the king's head, killing him with his own weapon.

When Ring heard that Harald was dead, he ordered his men to stop fighting. He then made a truce with the defeated Danes, saying that it was meaningless to carry on fighting now that their king had been slain. Ring ordered that Harald's body must be found so that the old king could be honoured. Many thousands of men had fallen that day on both sides. So the bodies of many dead men had to be turned over, and it was some time before the king's corpse was found together with the club that had killed him.

Harald was given a funeral worthy of a great king, and his body was burnt on a pyre along with the gilded chariot and many other valuable things.

* * *

For notes, see page 167

FRIDLEIF and the DRAGON

Soon after Fridleif had won his bride, he was sailing home, and one night he dreamed a dream. An old man appeared to him as he slept, and the man told him this:

"There is an island not far from here, and on that island there is a dragon. The dragon is guarding a great treasure that lies buried there. You should land on this island and kill the dragon, then you will get the treasure. But listen to what I say. The dragon has a fierce bite, and it spits poison from its mouth. You should wear oxhide to protect yourself from the poison, and also use a shield covered in oxhide."

Then the man vanished, and Fridleif woke up. Fridleif believed that what he had heard in the dream would come to pass. So he sailed to that island.

As he landed on the shore, Fridleif saw the dragon rise up out of the waves. It was a huge beast. As it writhed its way forward across the land, its body left a trench in the earth, and either side of this banks of earth were thrown up. The coils of the dragon's tail knocked over trees, so wherever it went it left a trail of destruction behind it.

Fridleif attacked the dragon first with spears and arrows. He struck the dragon many times, but the missiles just bounced off the dragon's back as the scales that covered it were as hard as horn.

When Fridleif saw that it was useless to attack the upper part of the creature, he attacked it from below. He easily plunged his sword into the dragon's belly. Then the dragon was dead.

After that, Fridleif dug deep into the hill and found the treasure that was buried there. He took it back to his ships, and then he continued on his way home.

FRODE and the DRAGON

Soon after Frode became king, a man came to him, and he sang this verse:

I have heard of an island, not far from here,
And high in the hills there, gold is hidden.
A precious hoard, proudly guarded,
By a dark dragon, the old mound dweller.

Its curling body, is coiled and folded,
With winding tail, and poisoned tongue.
Listen now, and learn from my words,
And better you'll be able, to beat that dragon.

Cover your shield, with the hides of cattle,
Under oxskins, shelter your body.
Safeguard yourself, from the sour spit,
Burning poison that destroys all it touches.

Though the forked, tongue will flicker,
And though the gaping, mouth will threaten,
You must stay strong, and steadfast in mind.

Do not fear, the force of that dragon,
Its poisonous drool, or its dreadful bite.

> Its scaly skin, will withstand your spears,
> The hide on its back, is as hard as horn.
> But there is a place, where the blade will plunge.
>
> Bury your sword, in the belly of the beast,
> Where its skin, is soft and supple.
> That dire dragon, will meet its death.
>
> Then climb the hill, and clamber through the cliffs.
> Dig deep, and discover the gold.
> Take for yourself, from the secret store,
> And carry the treasure, to your ships on the shore.

Frode was pleased when he heard the man's words, and he believed things would happen just as the man had sung.

So Frode sailed to that island. He went alone, because he felt it would not be right to attack the dragon with more men. And then he lay in wait. After some time, the dragon came out of its lair, and came down to the water to drink. Frode leapt up and threw spears at the dragon, but they simply bounced off its back. He stuck the dragon with his sword, but the blade didn't bite. The dragon's skin was too hard.

When he saw how hard the dragon's back was, Frode turned instead to the underside. He thrust his sword deep into the soft belly, where it entered easily. The dragon turned on Frode, and it tried to attack with bites and poison. But Frode protected himself with a shield covered in oxhide. The dragon's tongue flickered a little, but then it was still, and the dragon was dead.

Frode went up to the dragon's lair, and there he found a great deal of treasure. So Frode was very rich after that.

* * *

For notes, see page 168

AMLETH

There was a certain Horwendil who served under King Rorik. Horwendil was a great warrior and a fierce fighter. He served the king well, and always gave him the best of the treasures he won in war. That way he won favour with the king, and the king gave his daughter to Horwendil to marry. The king's daughter was called Gerutha, and Horwendil and Gerutha had a son who was called Amleth.

Horwendil's brother was called Feng. Feng grew very jealous of Horwendil, and he wanted to take everything he had for himself. So Feng treacherously murdered his brother. He wondered then how he might get Gerutha for himself, so he went to speak to her.

"Dear lady," he said to her. "My brother hated you very much. He didn't respect you and he treated you dishonourably. When I found out about this, I killed him at once."

The lie worked. Gerutha believed what Feng told her, and she took him as her husband.

Amleth saw everything that had happened, and he was well aware of the danger that he was in. He feared for his own life, so to protect himself he started to behave as though he was mad, or a fool. Amleth stayed in his mother's house all day every day. He was lazy, and he didn't wash. He rolled in the dirt on the floor, and he raked his hands through the ashes in the hearth and smeared the ash on his body. His face was pale and covered in mud. Anyone who saw him thought at once that he looked like a madman. He also made sure that everything he said fitted in with the illusion of madness, and that everything he did seemed pointless. But all the time he was thinking about how he could avenge his father and planning how he might kill Feng.

Amleth sat beside the fire, and with a knife he carved sticks to make little wooden hooks with pointed ends. He hardened the tips in the embers. Everyone was curious about what he was doing, and when they asked him, Amleth said: "With these sharp spears I will avenge my father." The answer sounded ridiculous, so they all laughed at Amleth and let him be.

But there were some of Feng's men who looked closely at what Amleth was doing. They saw the high level of craftsmanship when he worked with his hands, and the skill he showed in his carving. And they saw how closely he guarded the stash of wooden hooks that he had made. "Surely a madman could not carve so well," they said. And some of them started to believe that Amleth was not as mad as he seemed to be.

They went to speak to Feng about it. He hardly believed that Amleth could be pretending to be mad, but he said: "We will test young Amleth and find out whether he is truly out of his mind. Take him to the forest, and take a girl as well. Let Amleth find the girl. If he does what any sane man would do with the girl, then we will know that he is not mad at all. But if he leaves her be, we will know that he is a fool."

Feng's men said they would do it. But there was one of Feng's men who had been fostered together with Amleth when they were both boys. He was a good deal more loyal to his fosterbrother than he was to Feng, so he went to warn Amleth about what was being planned.

"They will take you to the forest and you will find a girl there. But whatever you do you should not lie with her. If Feng finds out that you have done that then he will no longer believe that you are mad."

Amleth thanked his friend, and he made sure he was acting as foolishly as he could when Feng's men came to fetch him to take him to the forest. When Amleth came to mount his horse, he climbed on backwards so that the horse's head was behind him. He grabbed the tail as though it was the reins, and tried in vain to control the horse as it ran away.

While they were riding in the forest, a wolf crossed their path.

"Oh, did you see, Amleth, that little horse?" Feng's men laughed.

Amleth said: "I know many of those creatures fight in Feng's army." Amleth wanted to sound as foolish as he could, but he didn't want to tell a lie.

Before long, they came to the sea shore, and as they were riding along the sand, they came to where the rudder of an old ship was lying on the ground.

"Can you see that huge knife, Amleth?" Feng's men asked, laughing.

Amleth said: "A knife that size would surely cut deep." It sounded like a silly answer, but of course when he said deep, Amleth meant the sea.

As they rode further on, they came to an area that was covered in sandhills.

"Can you see the big piles of flour, Amleth?" Feng's men joked again.

Amleth said: "Those big piles must have been milled by swirling ocean storms." And of course it sounded silly, but Amleth wanted to give the best answer he could.

So they rode into the forest, and when they came to a certain place, they stopped and left Amleth alone. Before too long, the girl appeared. But Amleth's fosterbrother wanted to remind him to beware of the trap, so he sent a signal to Amleth: he attached a piece of straw to a fly, and then let the fly fly over to where Amleth and the girl were.

Amleth saw the fly, and he understood that it was a trap. Nevertheless, he was of course quite in his right mind, so he was overcome by desire for the girl he had found there in the forest. So he took her by the hand and the two of them went together deeper into the forest to some marshland. They went into the middle of the marsh where it would be hard for anyone to follow them and hard for anyone to see them, and there they lay together.

Now Amleth already knew this girl well as they had also been fostered together, and he trusted her. "Tell no-one what we did here," he told her. And she agreed.

When they had all returned home, Feng's men began to question Amleth.

"Did you find anything good to do in the forest?" they asked him.

"I found a girl there, and we lay together," Amleth said.

The men were surprised to hear him say it, and they could hardly believe it. "So where did you lie with her?" they asked him.

"We did it on a colt's foot, and then on a cock's comb, and then on straw thatch," Amleth said.

When they heard this, Feng's men started to laugh, as they realised that Amleth was talking nonsense as usual. They thought he was truly a fool and a madman. But Amleth was telling the truth in his ravings, for those three things are the names of plants that grow in marshland.

They also questioned the girl about what had happened. She declared that they certainly had not lain together, and as none of Feng's men had seen it happen, it made it easier to believe what the girl said.

Amleth's fosterbrother then wanted to give Amleth a hint that it had been him who had sent the fly as a warning sign. "I have been a good friend to you, Amleth," he said.

And Amleth said: "I saw a strange creature fly by with straw in its buttocks." It sounded ridiculous, and all Feng's men laughed. But Amleth's fosterbrother was reassured by what he heard.

* * *

So Amleth had managed to deceive them all, and Feng and his men were convinced that Amleth was as mad as he seemed. And yet still there were some who had doubts. One of the men went to Feng and said: "I believe that Amleth is cleverer than all of us. He is surely plotting against you, and yet he is here among us, hiding behind his pretended madness."

Feng said: "And do you have a better way of finding the truth about Amleth?"

The man said: "If there is one person here in this house who Amleth would dare to talk to openly, it is his mother. You should make some excuse and go away for some time. While you are gone, I will watch Gerutha closely in secret. And if Amleth comes to speak to her, I will be sure to listen to all that they say to each other."

So Feng told his wife that he had to go away for some weeks to visit an ally who lived far away, and then he left. The man went into Gerutha's room, and he hid himself there. There was a pile of straw on the floor of the room, and the man crawled under the straw and stayed there so that he could not be seen.

It was not long before Amleth came in to speak to his mother. At first he behaved in his usual foolish way. He walked around the room as though he was a rooster, crowing and flapping his arms like wings. He saw the straw, and he jumped up and down on it, all the way along, as though he was trying to fly. But really he was trying to see whether there was anyone hiding there. When he felt the lump under his feet where the man was hiding, he drew his sword and plunged it into the straw. And Amleth uncovered the man, who was now dead.

Amleth cut the dead man's corpse up into pieces, and boiled the meat until it was tender. Then he threw the pieces down into the sewer where the pigs were, and let the pigs eat up the remains of the man. Then Amleth returned to his mother.

She cried out when she saw him: "Foolish boy, what have you done?"

But Amleth spoke plainly to his mother: "What are you saying now? Do you think that by finding fault with me you will hide your own guilt? Or have you completely forgotten your first husband now that you have happily married his murderer? You must know that there is a good reason that I am pretending to be a madman and acting like a fool. A man who has murdered his own brother would hardly shy away from doing the same to his brother's son. A show of madness may offer me some protection from such a man. It is often necessary to use mind games when facing such a dark opponent. But you may know that I have sworn that I will avenge my father. I am waiting for my chance, and when the time comes I will take it!

"It would be better for you to recognise the fault in your own behaviour than to try to blame me. It is surely you and not me who has been acting like a true fool."

When Gerutha heard what Amleth had to say, and she realised what was happening, she knew that she had to help her son with whatever he was planning to do.

* * *

Feng returned home after a few weeks, and he tried to find the man who was supposed to be watching Amleth and Gerutha. But no matter where he looked, he could not find that man, and no matter who he asked, no-one knew where he had gone. Feng even asked Amleth as a joke whether he had seen the man. He hardly expected that the madman would have anything sensible to say.

"Yes I saw him," Amleth said. "He slipped and fell into the sewer. He died covered in filth, and the pigs ate up his body." It sounded ridiculous, and yet it was also the truth.

By now, Feng was convinced that Amleth was a danger for him. He wanted very much to kill him, but he was too afraid to do it himself. He was afraid that if he killed Amleth, his wife Gerutha would not like it at all, and her father King Rorik would not like it either. So he decided that he would send Amleth abroad to an ally, and let someone else do the killing. That way he could pretend that he knew nothing about it. And he hardly cared if people thought badly about his allies as a result of what he had done.

* * *

So Feng said to Amleth: "I would like you to travel to visit the King of Britain on my behalf. I will send two men to travel with you."

But when Amleth had gone, Feng said to two of his men: "Go with Amleth to Britain, and when you get to the king, give him this message. I think the problem of Amleth will go away after that." And Feng gave them a piece of wood on which he had carved runes.

The runes said this: "I am sending you this young man who has been a traitor. You should put him to death."

Before Amleth left for Britain, he went to speak to his mother. He said this to her: "I am sure Feng means to have me killed on this trip, but I will return in one year's time. Do this for me: while I am away, you should make a wall hanging, big enough to cover all four walls of Feng's hall. As I will be away for a year, you should have enough time to do it."

So Amleth and the two men went away. But one night while the men were asleep, Amleth found the message carved on the wood. He read what was written there, and understood what Feng had planned. Then Amleth scraped off the runes Feng had carved, and he carved his own message, telling the King of Britain that his two companions were the ones who were to be killed. He also added a request that the King of Britain should give his daughter in marriage to the wise young man who had come to him, and he signed the message with Feng's name. Then he put the piece of wood back where he had found it.

* * *

When they arrived at the court of the King of Britain, Feng's men handed the message to the king. They thought it told the king to kill Amleth, but in fact it told him to kill them. The king read the message. The guests were all well received, and on the first evening they went to eat in the hall.

Amleth and Feng's men were given the seats of honour, and many plates of fine food were brought out and set before them, and also drink. Feng's men ate heartily, and enjoyed the food that was offered to them. But Amleth hardly touched it. He sent the food back uneaten. And no matter what the king offered, he refused it all.

Everyone thought it was strange that anyone should refuse such fine food, especially such a young man, and a foreigner. Later that night, the king was speaking to his steward. He said: "I am curious as to why Amleth refused to eat or drink anything that we offered to him tonight. Go to the place where the guests will sleep, and see whether you hear them say anything that can give you an idea as to why he didn't eat the food."

So the Steward went, and he heard Amleth talking to Feng's men.

Feng's men said: "Why did you not eat any of the food that was offered you? Do you not see that it is considered rude? The king will surely be offended."

Amleth said: "The food was not as good as you think. The bread tasted of blood, and the beer tasted of iron. The ham stank of dead human flesh. But there is more. The king looked to me like a slave, and his queen acted like a servant girl. That was why I didn't eat the food."

Feng's men laughed because Amleth seemed to be talking nonsense as usual. But the steward returned to the king and told him what he had heard Amleth say.

The king said: "This young man is either very foolish or very wise. But I don't know which. What he says sounds ridiculous, but we should try to see whether there is any truth in it. So tell me, who made the bread that was served tonight?"

The steward said: "Your own baker made the bread."

The king said: "And where did the flour come from?"

The steward said: "I grew the corn myself that was milled to make the flour."

The king said: "And where did you grow the corn?"

The steward said: "I grew the corn in a field not far from here. It was a battlefield, and many men were slain there. I thought it would be a good place to grow corn, but I see now that perhaps the taste of the blood of the men who died was in the corn, and has polluted the bread."

Then the king said: "And how about the beer? Where did it come from?"

The steward said: "I brewed the beer myself."

And the king said: "And where did the water come from that you used to brew the beer."

The steward said: "That water came from a certain spring. But it is true that when I dug down into the spring, I found the remains of several old swords that had been thrown there, all rusty. I suppose the taste of that old metal could have got into the beer."

And then the king said: "And now tell me where the ham came from that was served tonight."

The steward said: "That ham came from your own pigs."

The king said: "And is there some way that the ham could have come to taste of human flesh?"

The steward said: "It is true that there were some robbers who were killed on the road near here, and the pigs wandered away from their sty and ate up the bodies. So I suppose it might be possible to taste those dead men in the meat."

Then the king said: "It seems that this Amleth is very wise indeed, although he seems foolish. But I am now worried about what he said about me and my wife."

The old king, who was the king's father, had died, but his mother was still alive and living there at the court. So the king went to speak to her. "Tell me," he said. "Was the old king really my father?"

"Of course he was your father," she said to him. "I didn't lie with anyone except the king."

Then the king said to his mother: "I mean to have the truth out of you. And if you do not tell me yourself, I will take this to a public trial."

When his mother heard this, she changed her story. "It is true that I also slept with a slave," she said. "And it is that slave who is your father, and not my husband."

So the king saw that Amleth had been right also about that matter. When he had heard all these things, the king went to speak to Amleth. "Why did you say these things about my wife?" he asked him. "Why did you say that she acted like a serving maid?"

Amleth said: "Your wife showed herself to act like a serving maid in three ways. First, she covered her head with her robe. Second, she picked up her robe when she walked so that it didn't drag along the ground. Third, she picked out pieces of food that were stuck in her teeth, and then she ate them."

The king said: "It is true that when I met my wife she was a serving maid. But I didn't know that it was so plain for others to still see this in her. You are truly a wise man."

The king and Amleth got on well after that, and the king promised at once that Amleth could marry his daughter. The king seized Feng's two men as he had been instructed in the message, and he put them to death. But Amleth pretended that he was not happy that the king had killed his two companions, and so the king offered him a generous amount of gold as compensation. Amleth had the gold melted down, and then he hid it inside two hollowed out logs. Amleth stayed with the King of Britain for a year after that.

When the year had passed, Amleth told the king that he would like to return to Denmark. So he took the two logs with the gold, and he left.

* * *

As soon as Amleth reached Denmark, he began again to act the fool, pretending to be mad. When Amleth reached Feng's hall, a great feast was being held, and it seemed to be a funeral feast.

Amleth said to one of the men there: "What is the meaning of this feast, or who has died?"

The man said: "It is Amleth, Feng's brother's son, who has died. He was killed in Britain, and this is his funeral feast."

But there were many there who recognised Amleth straight away. He appeared just as they were used to seeing him, covered in filth. And they were surprised to see him walk into his own funeral, quite alive. They called for Feng, and he came at once to see for himself.

"What happened to your two companions?" Feng asked.

Amleth said: "They have come back with me. Here is one, and here is the other." And he pointed at the two logs that he had brought with him. It sounded ridiculous, but it was not far from the truth. Because the two logs contained the gold that had been given as compensation for the deaths of the two men, and that was in fact all that was left of them.

Amleth urged everyone to continue with the feast. So what had begun as Amleth's funeral continued as a celebration of his safe return. Amleth himself wandered among the guests, and he pricked his fingertips with his sword so that his fingers bled. When Feng's men saw him doing this, they said: "He is not safe with a sword." So they took the sword from him and nailed it into the sheath so that it could not be drawn. Then they gave it back to him.

Time drew on. All the men had been drinking heavily, and they started to lie down where they were and fall asleep. When Amleth saw this, he saw that the time was right to put into action what he had been planning for so long. First he went to fetch the hooked sticks that he had carved from the place where he had hidden them. Then he took down the huge wall hanging that his mother had made, and he threw it over the sleeping men where they lay all over the floor. They were drunk, wheezing and snoring, and quite unaware of what was happening around them. And so they were all caught like fish in a net. Amleth went around the edges of the wall hanging and fastened it down firmly to the floor using the supply of hooked sticks. None of the men who were trapped underneath the wall hanging could move at all. Then Amleth set fire to the hall. It quickly caught light, and all Feng's men were killed.

But Feng was not in the hall when this happened. He had already left the feast and gone to bed in his own room. So Amleth went there.

"Wake up, Feng," Amleth called out. "All your men are burning in the hall. Amleth has come with his hooks to help him, and now he will have his revenge on the one who killed his father."

Feng leapt up from his bed and tried to draw his sword. But Amleth had swapped Feng's sword with his own. The sword that Feng held in his hands was nailed fast in its sheath, and the sword could not be used. But Amleth drew his own sword and he cut Feng down. And so Amleth avenged his father, and it was done more through wit and cunning than through strength. By playing the fool, Amleth was able to make fools out of all those who didn't see his true purpose, and for this Amleth's name deserves to live on for a long time.

* * *

For notes, see page 168

TOKE

There was a man called Toke who served with King Harald Bluetooth. He was a loyal man, and very talented. But several of the king's men resented him because of his great skills.

One time there was a feast. Toke had been drinking, and he happened to boast to the men he was speaking to that he was such a good archer that he could shoot a single arrow with his longbow and hit an apple, no matter how small, placed on top of a pole some distance away.

Some of Toke's enemies overheard this, and they went at once and told the king what Toke had said.

And so the king called Toke to him. "I have heard about your boasting," the king said. "Let us see whether you can really shoot as well as you say you can. You will try to hit an apple some distance away, but instead of a pole, the apple will be placed on top of your son's head. If you fail to hit the apple with your first arrow, then this will cost your life."

Toke had no choice but to agree. But he was confident in his ability, and the fact that the apple would be placed on his son's head rather than on a pole only made him more sure that he would succeed.

So Toke's son was fetched, and the apple was placed on his head.

"Do not be afraid," Toke said to him. "Do not tremble at the thought of the arrow, or bow your head in fear. Stand up straight and true, but stand facing away from me so that you do not flinch when you see the arrow coming towards you."

So Toke's son stood quite still, and Toke walked the required distance to the place where he would shoot. Then he took three arrows from his quiver. He fitted one to his bowstring, and he let the arrow fly. The apple was cleaved cleanly into two pieces, which fell down from the boy's head onto the ground.

"That was well shot," said Harald. "But tell me, why did you take three arrows from your quiver when this trial was to be decided with a single arrow?"

"If I had missed the shot," Toke said, "and if I had killed my son, then I would have used these other arrows to take my revenge on you, Harald. I do not deserve to be punished, but you should be punished for your cruelty."

It was not long after Toke had overcome this trial that he had to face another.

One time, King Harald happened to be boasting about his skill in running on skis in the manner of the Finns. "If there is a better skier than me, I don't suppose he has yet been born," Harald said.

But Toke said: "I believe I can run at least as well as you on skis."

Harald was furious when he heard this. "Let us see whether you are as good a skier as you say you are. There is a mountain near here called Kullen, and you can show us your skills by skiing down the steepest slope of that mountain."

Toke could not refuse, though he knew that what the king was ordering him to do was very dangerous.

So Toke climbed to the top of Kullen, and he strapped the skis onto his feet. Then he set off down the steep face with the skis on his feet and a pole in his hand. The hill was so steep that even the thought of skiing down it would have made most men tremble with fear. Toke slid over the snow, and soon he was moving very quickly indeed. There were steep cliffs all over that slope. Toke kept his nerve and avoided them as best he could, keeping his skis on the snow. But there were more steep cliffs ahead of him.

Then Toke's skis struck a rock that was hidden under the snow. The wooden skis broke into pieces and came off his feet. Toke fell on his face in the snow and came to a stop. But the broken pieces of his skis skidded down over the snow and fell down the cliffs into the sea. By this stroke of fortune, Toke was able to escape with his life. If he had not been stopped by those rocks, he would surely have ended up dead in the sea at the bottom of the hill.

Toke made his way carefully down the mountain, and was picked up by a ship. After this, Toke believed that as long as he was with Harald he would never be safe. He saw that rather than rewarding him for his courage and bravery, the king would carry on giving him one dangerous challenge after another. So he went to serve Sven, who was Harald's son, and there he found his skills were better appreciated.

But the story that reached King Harald was different. Some fishermen found the broken pieces of ski in the sea, and when Harald saw these, he assumed that Toke had been killed in the descent. Toke was happy to let Harald believe that story.

* * *

For notes, see page 170

ALFHILD and ALF

There was a girl called Alfhild who was the daughter of a king. From a very young age, Alfhild was so determined that she should not arouse the interest and desires of men that she kept her face covered at all times. Her father was also keen to protect his daughter from the unwanted attentions of men, so he gave her two young snakes to look after. These snakes lived with Alfhild, and when they were fully grown they guarded her chamber. The king made it widely known that no man could go in to see Alfhild without first getting past the snakes. If any man tried to enter and failed, then he would lose his head, and the head would be impaled on a stake.

All this dissuaded many potential suitors. But there was one young man called Alf who thought differently. Alf said: "I will go now to visit Alfhild. I will kill the snakes that guard her, and I will win the maiden. The added danger does not put me off. Rather it makes this quest even more attractive. For the greater the danger that is overcome, the greater the glory that will be won."

Alf dressed himself in an animal skin soaked in blood to make sure the snakes would attack him. And then he went to the place where the maiden was. Alf picked a piece of red-hot steel from the fire and held it with tongs. And when the first snake slithered towards him, its jaws agape, Alf plunged the burning metal into its open mouth. Then the second snake attacked. It slid quickly across the floor towards Alf, but he thrust his spear deep into its gaping jaws. And so both the snakes were dead.

Then Alf went to see the king. "I have killed the snakes that were guarding Alfhild's chamber, and I have entered in," he said. "And now I would like to marry your daughter."

The king said: "It is true that you have done this, and I am pleased, because I can see that you are a good man. But I cannot allow any man to marry my daughter who she has not chosen herself, so you should go to speak to Alfhild about this."

But Alfhild's mother did not like this at all. She went to speak to her daughter. "Tell me, daughter, what you think of the man who has come here," she said.

Alfhild said: "I believe that Alf is the bravest of men, for he has dared to come here and kill the two snakes, all to reach me."

"That is not such a great deed," her mother said. "I see that you have had your head turned by this young man. But you should not choose to marry a man just because he is handsome and good-looking. You should judge him by his virtue."

So Alfhild was convinced by her mother's words that she should not marry Alf, and Alf had to leave with nothing.

But after all this had happened, many things changed for Alfhild. She completely changed her former outlook on life, and abandoned her shy behaviour. She cut out and sewed men's clothes for herself, and she went off to live as a viking warrior. She found many other maidens who were similarly minded, and she invited them to join her. She also found a viking crew who were mourning the loss of their leader, and she persuaded them to accept her as a new leader.

Alfhild and her crew sailed on many viking voyages after that. She raided and did many great deeds, and became very well known.

Alf heard about what had happened to Alfhild, and he resolved to chase after her. So Alf sailed long and often on the sea. He heard stories about what Alfhild had done and where she had been, but by the time he arrived in those places she had always already sailed on. But in the time he was chasing Alfhild, Alf had many adventures of his own.

One time, Alf was sailing at midwintertime when he came across a fleet of ships belonging to the blue men.

The sea was frozen solid, and all the ships became caught in the ice. They could not move, no matter how hard they smashed their oars into the frozen surface of the sea. Alf told his men that they should prepare to leave the ships and go out onto the ice. But he told them all to put on special shoes that allowed them to run surefootedly on the

ice. Then they stepped out onto the ice and started to go away from the ships.

When the blue men saw Alf's men leaving their ships behind, they thought they were shamefully fleeing. So they decided that they too would leave their ships to chase them and cut them down. But the blue men were wearing ordinary shoes, unsuitable for walking on ice. So when Alf's men turned to fight them, the blue men had great difficulty keeping a firm footing on the frozen surface. They slipped and slid, and fell often, and Alf's men easily beat them.

Alf sailed on, and further on. Soon they came close to Finland, not far from where Alf had heard that Alfhild had been seen.

He entered a narrow sound, and as his ships came around a corner, they reached the place where Alfhild's ships were lying at anchor. Alfhild thought that it would be better to attack first than wait to be attacked. Alf thought that it would be shameful to retreat, even though it seemed as though he was outnumbered.

So there was a great battle. Both sides fought fiercely. But as they fought against those vikings, Alf's men all marvelled at their beautiful bodies. They admired the soft skin and shapely legs of their enemies.

Alf boarded Alfhild's ship, and he fought and killed anyone who stood in his way. Alfhild's helmet was knocked off. As soon as he saw her, Alf recognised that it was Alfhild, who he had chased for so long. He realised then that this battle would be better fought with kisses than with weapons. So he called out to his men. They all put their spears away, and the women were handled more gently after that.

So Alf and Alfhild were married, and Alfhild gave up her viking ways.

* * *

For notes, see page 171

GRAM, GROA, and BESS

There was once a King in Denmark called Gram who was strong and wise. He was also dedicated to improving himself, both in his mind and his knowledge of the world and also in his physical prowess.

The King of Sweden at that time was called Sigtryg, and he had a daughter called Groa. News reached Gram that Sigtryg had promised his daughter in marriage to a giant. The thought of this marriage between a giant and a king's daughter disgusted Gram, and at once he made plans to go to Sweden to start a war, hoping that he might get to kill some giants.

When Gram reached Sweden, in order to frighten the local people he disguised himself as a giant. He dressed himself in goat skins, and he carried a wooden club, rough and heavy.

It happened that Groa and her handmaidens were out in the forest, on their way to some forest pools to bathe. Groa was riding, and the maidens were on foot. As they came down the road, they were shocked to see Gram coming the other way with Bess, the fiercest of his warriors. Of course it seemed that Gram was a giant, and Groa feared that it was the one who she was going to marry, coming to meet her. She dropped the reins of her horse in fright, and trembling, she began to sing:

> A giant is coming, the curse of our kingdom,
> Darkening the road, with his dreadful strides.
> Or is a gallant hero, going in disguise,
> As has often happened before?

Then Bess spoke:

> Listen up, maiden, to what I say to you,
> Riding high, on your horse's back.
> Don't hesitate to tell me, all I ask:
> What's your name, or what's your father's line?

Groa replied:

> Groa I am called, the king is my father,
> Glorious in blood, gleaming in armour.
> Now tell me at once, all I want to know,
> What's your name, or where have you come from?

Then Bess said:

> Bess is my name, bold in battle.
> My enemies tremble, when they hear I am near.
> I fight fiercely, against my foes,
> And often bathe, my arms in their blood.

Groa replied:

> Now answer me this, who is your leader?
> Whose are the banners, that you bring into battle?
> Who is the lord, whose orders you act on?
> Who is your master, who leads you to war?

Then Bess replied:

> Gram leads the army, angry in war:
> Against any force, he feels no fear.
> No swinging sword, nor swirling sea,
> Nor blazing fire, makes him afraid.

Groa said:

> Hurry back to your homelands, far away from here,
> Or Sigtryg will beat you, sure in his victory.
> Your cold corpses will be strung with cords,
> And hung high, for the hungry ravens.

Bess said:

> Why do you threaten us, with this dreadful death?
> We are hardly worried, about Swedish warriors.
>
> Before he breathes, his last breath,
> Gram will make, a ghost of Sigtryg.
> It was hardly to die, that Gram came here,
> But to send Sigtryg, soon to his death.

Groa replied:

> I will ride with great haste, to my father's house,
> I dare not dally, while your army advances,
> But I wish on you, waiting in the woods,
> Only death and downfall.

Bess replied:

> Don't be disheartened, when you hurry home,
> And don't, in your anger, wish us an awful death.
> For a hard-hearted woman, may later become a lover,
> It has often happened before.

When he heard this, Gram could no longer bear to be silent. He spoke to the maiden in a gruff voice, as a terrible and otherworldly creature might speak:

> Don't be afraid, maiden, of the fierce giant,
> And don't, when you see me, shudder with dread.
>
> For your sake, maiden, I made my way here,
> Driven on, by a dream of marriage,
> But I only enter, a woman's arms,
> When her wishes match my own.

Groa replied:

> Who is so mad, as to love a monster,
> Or what woman could want, to wed a giant?
> Who could embrace, such a brutal beast,
> Or who could kiss, such a coarse creature?

Such a love is hard, and tears at the heart,
For all of nature, knows it to be wrong.

Then Gram took off his disguise and revealed his true appearance. He replied, singing this verse in his own voice:

Many are the proud, kings I have killed,
And many the rulers, I have beaten in battle.
So take this gift, maiden, of reddest gold,
And see that you will have, a good husband in me.

And so Gram won Groa. But his business was not finished in Sweden, as he still had to fight against the maiden's father.

* * *

After this, Bess left Gram and Groa, and carried on down the forest road alone. Suddenly two robbers leapt out of the trees and attacked him. But Bess was a skilled warrior, and it was not long before the two robbers were lying dead on the ground.

But this presented a problem for Bess. He was abroad in the land of his enemies, and he had just killed two robbers. Bess was worried that in doing this he might be seen to have served his enemies well. Bess did not want this at all. He hated Sweden, and had no wish to help the people of that country, making the forest road safer for them to travel. So he cut down branches from trees and attached the pieces of wood to the corpses. Then he placed the dead men firmly fixed in an upright position in the road. That way, it would seem to anyone who tried to pass down the forest road that the robbers were standing there, still alive and guarding the road. And they could continue to threaten and frighten the people of Sweden even after their death.

Thus it was clear that in killing the robbers Bess acted only out of self-interest and not at all for the benefit of the Swedish people.

* * *

When King Sigtryg was young, a seeress had foretold that he would not be killed by steel, but that gold would bring about his downfall. So Sigtryg was happy to fight in many battles, confident that he would not die by the sword. He was always rather more careful in the way he dealt with wealth.

Gram had heard about the prophecy, and so when he went into battle against Sigtryg, he attached a golden ball to his club. Even though Gram did not have a sword, he fought well against the Swedes. He swung his club, and was able to beat off their swords and spears. And then he was able to fulfil the prophecy just as it had been foreseen. The one who could not be killed by steel was struck down and crushed by the noble gold of Gram's club.

And that is how Gram killed Sigtryg and became the King of Sweden.

* * *

For notes, see page 171

FRIDLEIF and the ROBBERS

I know of a river that flows in the Norwegian mountains. Many small streams tumble down from the high fells and come together to form this great river. It flows swift and deep. The river crashes against the many rocks that lie in its path, so the water foams white as milk, and spray is thrown high into the air. There are roaring waterfalls and swirling eddies, and that river is very hard to cross.

There is a place where the river widens and flows around a big rock on both sides. So that rock is an island in the middle of the river. It is very hard to reach that island, as it is difficult to swim across those fast, rough-flowing waters. Just there, the river flows at the bottom of a deep gorge surrounded on all sides by trees, so it is difficult to see that place from any distance away.

There were twelve brothers who came to live on that island. These are the names of some of them, I cannot remember them all: Gerbjorn, Gunbjorn, Arinbjorn, Stenbjorn, Esbjorn, Thorbjorn, and Bjorn. Those brothers were fierce warriors. They were brave and strong, and had won many victories over giants, and gathered a lot of treasure. But now they spent their time raiding the area surrounding the island. They made their base on that island as they knew it would be difficult for anyone to reach them there. Those brothers built a high wall on the island around their houses, and they also built a bridge across the river to reach the island. They could lower the bridge on ropes if they wanted to cross the river, but they could also raise it to stop anyone else coming across to the island.

The eldest of the brothers was called Bjorn. He had a horse that was counted among the best of horses. That horse could run very quickly,

and it could also swim across the rapids in the river to reach the island. Most animals that tried to swim there grew tired in the rough waters and were washed away and killed.

Bjorn also had a dog, and it was among the fiercest of dogs. Before, this dog had belonged to the giant Ofoot, who used it to guard his herds of sheep and goats on the fells. This fierce animal would often kill twelve men all by itself.

On their raids, those brothers did a great deal of damage, and they terrorised everyone who lived in the lands surrounding the river. They would rob houses, slaughter cattle, steal treasure, burn houses and destroy anything else they found, and kill men and women alike. So these brothers were not good to meet.

The king of that country was very troubled by these brothers. But he could not stop their behaviour. So he called upon a certain Fridleif, who was a king in exile, to help him.

"I would be happy to help you," Fridleif said.

One time, the brothers had ridden out raiding. But Fridleif was lying in wait. He surprised them, and they turned and fled back to the island as quickly as they could. But in the confusion, Bjorn left his horse behind, and Fridleif was able to take it.

Then Fridleif said to his men: "Anyone who kills one of these robbers will be rewarded with the dead man's weight in gold."

There were many men who answered eagerly that they would like to kill the robbers. But they were motivated just as much by the thought of the glory and honour that they would win by such a great deed as by the prize that Fridleif had offered. They said they would gladly risk their lives trying to kill the robbers.

But Fridleif didn't want it to seem that he relied on other men to do what he was too afraid to do himself. So said to them: "Wait here. I will go first with one slave and see how many of those robbers I can kill myself."

So Fridleif and the slave went down to the river by night. When they reached the water's edge, Fridleif picked up a stone, and he beat the slave to death. Then he changed their clothes so that he was wearing the dead man's clothes and the corpse was wearing his. Fridleif thought that if anyone found the body, they would think that it had been him who had been killed and not the slave. Then he threw the body into the river.

Fridleif also smeared the horse he had ridden there with blood, and he set it free so that it would walk back to the camp. That way, Fridleif thought that when the men saw the bloody horse walk back into the camp they would think that he had been killed.

Then Fridleif mounted Bjorn's hose, which he had also brought with him, and he rode out into the river. That horse swam easily across the channel, and soon it was climbing out of the water onto the island with Fridleif on its back. Unseen, he climbed up and over the wall that the brothers had built to surround that place, and was inside the enclosure. He made his way quietly over to the hall where the brothers were, and he sat down under the roof outside the door.

The brothers were sitting feasting in their hall. Even though they had been attacked that day, they thought they had little to worry about as they thought no-one would be able to reach them on the island. No-one could cross that fast-flowing river by swimming or fording.

But Bjorn said: "I dreamed I saw a monster climbing out of the water onto this island. Its eyes were glowing, and fire came from its mouth. I saw that fire spreading and burning everything. We should be careful not to become too complacent as overconfidence could lead to our downfall. I fear we may soon be attacked, and no place is so secure that it needs no defence at all."

So they agreed to search the island. They soon found Bjorn's horse. They were pleased to see the horse, so they opened the gate and let it in.

"It must have found its own way back and swum over to the island," they said. "And if anyone was riding this horse they would have been thrown off in the rough water and drowned."

Then the brothers stopped their search and returned to their feast.

Bjorn was still worried about the dream. "We must be on our guard," he said. And then he went to bed.

Meanwhile, the horse that Fridleif had covered in blood arrived back at the camp. When Fridleif's men saw it, they thought that Fridleif must have been killed.

The men all got onto their horses and rode down to the river as fast as they could. They found the slave's body where it had washed up on the riverbank, and when they saw that the body was dressed in Fridleif's clothes, they were sure that Fridleif must have died. The slave had been so badly beaten with the rocks that it was easy to make that mistake.

Those men had promised Fridleif that they would kill the robbers, and they did not want to go back on their word just because Fridleif was dead. They were now motivated just as much by their desire for vengeance for Fridleif.

When Fridleif saw the men on the other side of the river, he quickly lowered the bridge so that they could cross to the island. Fridleif's men saw that the bridge was down, and they rode across. They took the robbers by surprise, and they killed them all. All except for Bjorn. Fridleif let him live and made sure that his wounds were tended. Then he made him swear an oath of allegiance to him. He thought it would be better to have such a fierce warrior as Bjorn as an ally.

* * *

For notes, see page 171

The EVERLASTING BATTLE: HAGEN, HEDIN, and HILDA

There was once a chief's son called Hedin. This Hedin heard about a chief's daughter called Hilda, and he fell very much in love with her, though he had never seen her with his own eyes. At the same time, Hilda had also heard about Hedin, and she fell very much in love with him, though she had not seen him with her eyes either. When they did finally meet, they could not take their eyes off each other, they were so overcome by love.

Hilda's father was called Hagen. He was an unusually tall man, very stern, and very fierce. Hedin was very good-looking, but also short.

Winter passed and summer came, and summer was the season for viking raiding. Hedin and Hagen decided that they would go raiding together, and they swore an oath of brotherhood to one another such that if either one of them was killed, the other would avenge him. So they sailed together on many raids, and won a great deal of treasure. They also went to fight alongside King Frode in his war against the Huns. It is said that when the Huns were defeated, there were dead bodies strewn over such a wide area that it would take three days to ride across it. And there were so many bodies floating in the three main rivers in Russia that it was possible to cross any one of those rivers from one side to the other just by stepping on the dead men.

After they had raided and fought together for this time, Hagen was very pleased with Hedin, and he told him that he could marry his daughter, Hilda. Hagen did not know then that Hedin was already in love with Hilda, or that Hilda was already in love with Hedin.

But then someone started to spread the lie that Hedin and Hilda had already lain together before they were properly married. This was seen as a terrible thing. Hagen believed the story, and he was furious with Hedin. So he sailed to find Hedin, and he attacked him. Hedin fled.

King Frode heard about this disagreement between two of his leading warriors, and he was not happy. He summoned the two of them to him, and demanded that they explain themselves. When he had heard what they had to say, Frode tried to get Hagen and Hedin to agree to a peaceful solution. But they would not have it. The only way that they would be satisfied was if the argument was settled by fighting a duel.

So the two of them went to an island, and they started to fight. They fought for a long time, and neither of them seemed to have the upper hand. But then Hagen seemed to summon all his strength, he struck the younger man and gave him a big wound. Hedin started to bleed heavily, and he grew weak. But Hagen did not kill him. He was fond of Hedin, who was so young and strong and handsome, and he could not bring himself to destroy him. So Hedin's life was spared by the kindness of his enemy.

Seven years later, the two of them came back to fight a second duel in the same spot. And this time, things did not go as well for either of them. It would have been better for Hagen if he had killed Hedin while he had the chance. Hedin and Hagen were both badly wounded in this fight, and they both died.

But Hilda's love and longing for her husband was so great that every night she used magic to raise the spirits of Hedin and Hagen, so that every night they might continue their fight.

* * *

For notes, see page 172

HAGBARD and SIGNE

There was once a king called Sigar who had two sons and a daughter. The two sons were called Alf (who married Alfhild) and Alger, and the daughter was called Signe. Alf and Alger often sailed out on viking raids, while Signe stayed at home with her mother.

Alf and Alger were away sailing one time when they happened to meet a fleet of ships belonging to Hamund's sons. These were three brothers called Hagbard, Hamund, and Helwin, and all three of them were viking warriors. And so a great battle began. They all fought fiercely until the end of the day, and then when it started to get dark and they could no longer see they called a truce for the night.

But when morning came, they were all still tired from fighting the day before. Many men were wounded and many had been killed on both sides, and none of them wanted to start over again. So the two sets of brothers made peace with each other, and they all sailed back together to Sigar's house.

Now Hagbard knew that Alf and Alger had a sister, and he decided that he would go and meet her in secret without their knowledge. And so it was that Hagbard and Signe became lovers.

It happened that men would come to Sigar's house to court his daughter. And around this time, there was a certain Hildigisl who had come for that reason. Hildigisl was high-born and handsome, but Signe was not at all impressed.

"What has Hildigisl done in his life?" she said. "Everything he owns he has got through the work of others. Everything has been given to him, and he has earned nothing. What use are good looks if a man lacks spirit?"

Signe's handmaidens were very impressed by Hildigisl's good looks, so they said to her: "Who then would you rather have?"

"You have heard tell of Hakon the viking," Signe said. "His face may be weathered by the sea spray, and his skin stained with salt and scarred by battle wounds. But the spirit burns brighter inside him than any man who has stayed at home all his life.

"He is not handsome, but he has a bold heart. And the daring he shows in the great deeds he does more than makes up for any lack of good looks. The raw roughness of his face reflects his fierce spirit. Hakon's merits come not from his beauty but his bravery.

"It is true that Hildigisl has a pretty face and shining hair. But these are empty assets that will never last. Good looks will wither and fade, but honour and glory won through great deeds will live on for a long time.

"Many are fooled by a beautiful face, and forget to think about a man's true worth. But I think only of a man's spirit and his deeds, and have no interest in handsome men."

Everyone who heard what Signe said thought the same thing: although she used the name Hakon, she was really talking about Hagbard.

* * *

When Hildigisl found out that Signe was refusing him, and he heard what she had said about him, he was not pleased. He decided that he would try to stir up some bad feeling between Signe's family and Hagbard's family.

King Sigar had two advisors. They were two brothers called Bolwis and Bilwis, and both of them were old men. But the two brothers were very different from one another. Bilwis liked to resolve conflicts and come up with solutions to arguments that left everyone happy and satisfied. But Bolwis liked to spread discord, arouse suspicions among friends, and find reason for disagreement where there was none. Bolwis was also blind.

So Hildigisl went to speak to Bolwis: "I am not happy about the friendship between Sigar's sons and Hamund's sons," he said. "If you turn these men against each other and turn their friendship into hatred, then I will reward you with more gold than you can want."

Bolwis was very happy to help. He went to Alf and Alger at once, and began to whisper lies in their ears about Hamund's sons: "These men are untrustworthy," he said. "They are disloyal. If you try to form a friendship with them it will turn out badly for you. It would be better to crush them now before things get worse."

And so the trust was broken. Not long after that, Hagbard sailed away on a raid. And while he was gone, Alf and Alger attacked his two brothers. Helwin and Hamund were both killed in the battle. When Hagbard found out what had happened, he was furious. He did not hesitate, but returned at once with many men. He attacked Alf and Alger, and killed them both. Hildigisl was also at that battle. He was wounded by a spear in the buttocks, and so many people mocked him after that.

After the battle, Hagbard thought about how he might go to speak to Signe. It was unthinkable that he could walk back into Sigar's house having just killed his two sons. But he wanted to see Signe very much, and he was sure that she would remain loyal to him. So Hagbard disguised himself as a woman.

He said this when he arrived at the house: "I am one of the viking women who sail with Hakon. And I have come with a message for Sigar."

So Hagbard was allowed into the house, and at night, he was taken to the women's hall to sleep with the women. The maid who was washing Hagbard's feet said to him: "Why are your legs so hairy, or why are your hands not soft to touch?"

Hagbard said: "It is hardly any wonder that the soft soles of my feet should harden and my legs grow shaggy with hair. I have walked a long way on the sea shore, and tangled many times with briars in the forest. I have run through the forest and sailed on the sea, and I have fought in many battles. I have not worn smooth gowns, but steel armour that has hardened my breast. My hands have not held distaffs, but bloody spears. Is it any wonder that my skin is harder than yours?"

And Signe supported Hagbard. She said: "When warrior women sail with Hakon the viking, their skin is stained by the salt spray. The soles of their feet grow tough and horny from walking on shingle shores. And their hands harden from pulling on oars and ropes."

So Hagbard and Signe slept together that night. While they were enjoying each other's company, Hagbard said: "I fear your father will soon take me and have me put to death. When I am dead, will you ever forget our love, or will you ever hope to marry again?

"If your father finds me, I can hardly hope for mercy. For I slew both his sons, and he will surely want revenge for that. And now I am lying in bed with his daughter. So tell me, my love, what will you do when I am gone?"

Signe said: "If it happens that you die before me, then I will not want to live any longer. If death takes you soon to your grave, then I want to die with you."

Hagbard was delighted when he heard this. The thought that Signe was ready to die with him brought such pleasure that it easily out-weighed any fear he might feel of his own death.

But a false maidservant betrayed them in the night. She rushed with news to Sigar: "The woman who came here yesterday is no woman. It is Hagbard himself, and he is now sleeping with Signe."

The king roared out to all his men, and ordered them to go and take Hagbard at once. So Hagbard was disturbed as he lay in bed. He heard the men approaching, and he leapt up. He grabbed his sword, and struck many of them down in the doorway as they tried to enter the room. But there were too many men, and soon Hagbard was taken prisoner and brought before the king.

The king asked his two advisors, Bolwis and Bilwis, what they thought should be done about Hagbard. "He has killed my two sons, and now I find that he has come in disguise into my house to sleep with my daughter!"

Bilwis always spoke in favour of the resolution of conflicts and positive and peaceful solutions to problems. "It is clear that Hagbard is a great warrior," he said. "It would be better to make an ally of him. Take him into your service, and let him marry Signe, and I am certain that he will serve you well."

But his brother Bolwis had a different idea. "The crimes this man has committed against you are inexcusable," he said. "There is no way he can be pardoned. Let your righteous anger steer your thoughts rather than misguided pity. To spare this man would make you seem weak and indecisive. Hagbard must pay at once with his life."

Everyone who heard Bilwis and Bolwis speak had a different view on what should happen to Hagbard. Some thought that the king should pardon him and make him his ally. Others thought that he should be given the harshest punishment. But the king chose to go with Bolwis's advice. "He will be hanged," he said. "Take him to the hill."

The queen then handed Hagbard a cup of wine. "Drink this," she said, "shameless boy, now that the hour of your death has come. Taste the wine, knowing that soon you will leave your life behind. Only the underworld awaits you now."

Hagbard took the cup, and he said: "This hand that now holds the cup is the same hand that struck down your two sons. Yes I will taste a last taste, and drink a last drink. I do not go to the underworld unavenged. By taking your sons' lives I have already wounded you. The children that you brought into the world were not spared by my deadly sword. You are left a childless mother, luckless and hopeless, wild in your mind. You rob me of my future, but I have also taken yours."

So Hagbard was not repentant towards the queen, even at the end. He taunted her with the thought that he had killed her children, and he threw the wine from the cup into her face, drenching her with it.

When Signe heard what was going to happen to Hagbard, she said this to her handmaidens: "Are you prepared to join me in doing what I plan to do?"

"We will do whatever you want us to do," they said.

Signe said: "I want to die along with the only man I ever loved. As soon as I see that he has lost his life, we will all hang ourselves by the neck inside this house using ropes made from our dresses, and we will also burn the house down."

The maidens agreed. Then Signe gave them some wine to make their deaths easier to bear.

Standing by the gallows on the hill, Hagbard wanted to test the loyalty of his lover. So he spoke to the hangman: "Will you hoist my cloak up so that I can see what is going to happen to me?"

The hangman hung Hagbard's cloak up on the gallows. But from where Signe was watching in the house down below, it seemed as though it was Hagbard himself who was hanging there. As soon as she saw it, she gave the word to her handmaidens. They torched the house so that it quickly burst into flame, and they kicked away the wooden bench from under their feet so they were all hanging by their necks.

Up on the hill, Hagbard saw the house burning, and he knew that his lover had killed herself. In this way, he found it easier to face his own death. He told the hangman he was ready.

"Hang me up now," he said. "It is sweet to die when my bride is dead before me. I see the hall burning, and the flames licking the rooftop. I see my woman has kept her word, and now she shares my death as she shared my life before. So let me hang. Let the rope hold my neck. I will know happiness again, for even in the underworld love does not die, and soon our souls will stay together."

And then they hung Hagbard up, and soon he was dead. And that is how both Hagbard and Signe died.

* * *

For notes, see page 172

RAGNAR and LADGERDA

There was a king of Sweden called Fro, and one time, this king attacked Norway. He killed the king, and forced many of the noblewomen to work as prostitutes.

At this time, Ragnar was the King of Denmark. He was outraged when he heard what had happened, and he was determined to travel to Norway and take revenge on King Fro for the way those women had been humiliated. There were many Norwegian women who heard about what Ragnar was doing for the sake of their kinswomen. They cut out and sewed men's clothes for themselves and came to fight alongside him. Ragnar was very happy to accept the help of those whose honour he had come to avenge.

One of these women would always fight furthest forward in the ranks, among the fiercest of the men. She was a skilled warrior, as brave as any man. She let her hair hang freely over her shoulders as she fought. Everyone who saw her was surprised, because they saw how fearlessly she fought, and yet they could also see from her long hair that she was a woman.

Ragnar saw this warrior woman fighting, forward in the fray, and after the Swedish king had been defeated, he said this to his men: "This victory was surely won thanks to this woman. Tell me, who is she?"

"Her name is Ladgerda," they told him, "and she is the daughter of a nobleman."

So Ragnar sent word to Ladgerda, asking for her hand in marriage. Ladgerda was not inclined to accept, but she pretended to be interested, and she invited Ragnar to come and visit her at her home. But she placed two wild animals outside her house, a dog and a bear, so that they would guard the entrance, and attack and kill anyone who tried to come in.

When Ragnar heard that Ladgerda had agreed to meet him, he sailed to Gaulardale. Then he left his men with the ship, and walked on to Ladgerda's house alone.

When he approached the house, the two beasts attacked him. But Ragnar was able to defend himself. He throttled one of them to death, and drove a spear through the heart of the other. And then he was able to enter Ladgerda's hall.

And so Ragnar won the maiden Ladgerda. The two of them were married, and they lived together in peace for some time after that.

* * *

For notes, see page 173

RAGNAR and THORA

There was once a King of Sweden called Herod, and he had a daughter called Thora. One day, when he was out hunting, this king found two young snakes, and he brought them home for his daughter to rear. He thought that the snakes might protect her from any unwanted attention.

So Thora looked after the snakes. She was happy to do it. She didn't know then what trouble those snakes would bring to the country. She fed them every day, and they grew bigger and bigger. Soon those two snakes were each eating a whole ox carcase every day.

The snakes took to roaming about the countryside, and everywhere they went they left destruction behind them. Trees were knocked down, and crops were destroyed. So the king offered a great reward to anyone who could rid the country of this pest: "The man who kills these two snakes will have my daughter's hand in marriage."

Many men heard about this, and the thought of the glory and honour they would win by such a great deed gave at least as much motivation as the thought of winning the maiden. But all the warriors who came to fight the snakes were themselves killed.

Ragnar also heard about this, and he thought that it would be a worthy challenge to fight the snakes. He was also growing tired of his wife, Ladgerda. He knew that he could never completely trust her, as he could not forget that she had tried to kill him with a dog and a bear. So Ragnar divorced Ladgerda, and set his heart on winning Thora instead.

Ragnar came up with a plan to beat the snakes, and he went to see his nurse. "I need some clothes," he said. "Very hairy, but light enough that I can move freely in them."

So Ragnar's nurse made him a woollen cloak and woollen trousers, both very hairy. And wearing these clothes, Ragnar set off.

When Ragnar came close to the house where Thora was, it was midwinter, and the air was very cold. He plunged his whole body, fully clothed, into a pool of water. When he stood on the land again, the clothes froze hard. Ragnar thought it would be hard for those snakes to harm him while he was protected by these frozen clothes. He also tied his sword to his side, and tied a spear to his right hand.

As he approached the house, a huge snake slid across the ground towards him, and a second followed just behind. They spat poison from their gaping jaws, but the poison was repelled by the frozen clothes. They tried to bite him, but the icy cloak and trousers protected Ragnar. They tried to coil their bodies around him to crush him, but Ragnar fought back.

The king's men saw what was happening from where they were standing by the castle. But they all hid. None of them came to help Ragnar. They were all too afraid of the snakes. So Ragnar fought alone.

And thanks to his fierce strength and also to the protection offered by his icy cloak and trousers, Ragnar was able to beat the snakes. No matter how much poison they spat from their mouths, it could not get through his frozen clothes. Ragnar struck with his spear. He drove it through the hearts of both of the beasts, and they were dead.

When the king saw that Ragnar had killed both the snakes, he came out from where he was hiding. He wondered at the frozen hairy clothes that Ragnar was wearing. He was particularly fascinated by his trousers. So the king gave Ragnar the nickname Lodbrok, which means hairy trousers.

And that is how Ragnar won Thora.

* * *

For notes, see page 173

RAGNAR and ESBJORN's DAUGHTER

Ragnar happened to fall very much in love with a certain maiden, who was the daughter of a man called Esbjorn. Ragnar treated Esbjorn very well, and in this way he hoped that he might win his favour. He invited him to many feasts, and let him sit next to him in the seat of honour. He also gave him fine gifts.

Esbjorn wondered for a while why Ragnar was treating him so well. Then he thought that perhaps it was because he was in love with his daughter. But Esbjorn was not pleased when he realised what was going on, and that this pretended kindness was part of a scheme. He guarded his daughter ever more closely and did not allow anyone to see her.

But Ragnar suspected that the daughter looked more kindly on his advances than her father did, and so he thought of a plan whereby he might get close to her. Ragnar went to a farmer's cottage close to where the girl lived, and there he swapped his clothes for women's clothes.

Wearing this disguise, he approached the maiden's hall, and was admitted at once. To better play the part and to avoid suspicion, he set to doing women's work, spinning wool, though his hands and fingers were hardly suited to it. And when night came, he was able to sleep in that girl's embrace.

It happened that the girl became pregnant, and as the months drew by, her condition became clear to her father.

"How has this happened?" he asked her. "Who have you been sleeping with? Was it a warrior, or was it a servant?" But no matter how many times he asked her, he was never satisfied with her answer.

"I have had no-one in my bed but my handmaid," the girl told him.

Esbjorn was unwilling to punish an innocent maidservant on a charge that was so clearly false, so he did nothing. And soon Ragnar's son was born.

* * *

For notes, see page 173

The DEATH of RAGNAR

Ragnar became a great warrior, he won many victories, and he was feared by all his enemies. He also became the ruler over many lands. This is the story of how he died.

There was a king called Ella. Ella heard about how Ragnar had refused to accept Christianity and was encouraging the old religion. Ella was furious about this, so he attacked Ragnar, and Ragnar was defeated.

Ella took Ragnar prisoner, and he threw him into a snake pit with poisonous snakes. Those snakes ate his liver, and were about to start to eat his heart. But when Ragnar saw that he was about to die, he started to speak. He told of all the great deeds he had done in his life, and finally he said these words: "When they hear about the boar's predicament, the piglets will surely hurry back to the sty."

Ella heard what Ragnar said, and he realised that some of Ragnar's sons must still be alive. He grew very afraid. He ordered his men to go to the snake pit at once and take away the snakes. But when they got there, Ragnar was already dead.

So Ragnar had mixed fortunes. He was a powerful viking, unbeaten in battle, and he ruled over a great empire. And yet he lost his power, his men were killed, and he was killed by beasts in the prison of his enemy. In the end, the heart that had been so strong in the face of so many dangers was eaten by poisonous snakes. So no man should trust too much in fortune.

* * *

When Bjorn heard the news about his father's death, he was playing dice. He gripped the dice so hard that blood burst from his fingers and fell onto the table. Bjorn said: "Fortune is more fickle than the cast of a dice."

When Siward heard the news about his father's death, he plunged a spear into his own foot. He said: "This physical pain is easier for me to bear than the pain I feel from the loss of my father. The aching in my heart is greater than anything I feel from my own body." By inflicting this pain on himself, he thought he would be better able to bear the pain of loss. And so he showed that he was both brave and loyal.

When Ivar heard the news about his father's death, he was watching sports. He showed no feelings of sorrow at all, and no sign of any emotion. He also said that no-one who was there at the sports must show any distress, and he didn't allow anyone to leave. The competitors had to continue to compete, and the show had to go on. Ivar did not allow the spirit of the event to change from merriment to mourning, and so he behaved less like a bereaved son and more like a proud leader.

Ella heard about how Ragnar's sons had reacted when they got the news of their father's death. He thought the news had been borne most bravely by the one who had shown no sign of distress. And so Ivar was the one he feared the most.

* * *

For notes, see page 173

FRODE and FROGER

There was once a king called Frode who was very strong, but also very wise. Frode wanted to fight another king who was called Froger. This Froger was a good fighter and a fearsome warrior. He had won many victories in battle, and he had become very rich. In fact, Froger was Odin's son, and it was said that he could never be defeated in battle unless his opponent could pick up the earth from beneath his feet as they fought. So Frode thought that if he was going to defeat Froger, it would have to be through cunning rather than through strength.

So Frode challenged Froger to a duel, and Froger accepted this challenge. But when they came to the place, Frode said to Froger: "Great king, I am very young, and have fought few fights. I wonder whether you could teach me something about the art of fighting. Because I know that you are a skilled warrior, and have won many battles."

Froger said: "You are wise to come here and ask me this. It is true that I have won many victories. I can see that you are not battle-scarred, and that you have much to learn."

So they went out onto the field, and Froger showed him the way things usually went. Froger traced out two squares on the ground, each with sides about four feet long. Then he gave Frode certain tips about how he might fight within the areas marked out.

Frode seemed happy enough with this explanation, and each of them took his position in one of the squares. But when the time came for them to start to fight, Frode said: "Could we swap places, and could we swap weapons?"

Froger didn't see anything wrong with this. Frode had brought with him a magnificent sword with a gold hilt, and bright and shining armour, and a hard helmet, decorated with fine patterns. Froger thought that all those things looked better than his own, and he wanted to have them very much. So he agreed to swap.

So Froger went to stand in Frode's place, and Frode went to Froger's place. But as they stood there, Frode reached down and picked up a handful of earth from the place where he was now standing, which is to say from the place where Froger had stood. When Froger saw this, he knew that he would be beaten that day.

And he was not mistaken. When Frode attacked Froger, he slew him at once. And so by this trick, Frode was able to win a great victory. And using his wisdom, he was able to achieve what no man had achieved by strength alone.

*　*　*

For notes, see page 174

Notes

1–3. HOTHER, NANNA, and BALDER; The DEATH of BALDER; and VENGEANCE for BALDER (from Book III)

The story of Balder told here in Chapters 1–4 is probably the closest Saxo comes to telling a complete story that is recognisably parallel to any of the Icelandic stories of the Norse gods. There are a great number of similarities: Balder is in love with Nanna, Balder has bad dreams, Balder is killed by Hother (*Hod* in Icelandic sources), Odin fathers a son by Rinda who will avenge Balder. And yet the details of the two versions of the story are very different indeed.

In the Icelandic story, all the characters are gods, but in Saxo's story all are human except for Balder, who is a demigod, and Odin, who is a god (other gods including Thor come to fight alongside Balder in one of the battles). In the Icelandic story, Balder and Nanna are happily married, but in Saxo's story it is Hother and Nanna who are in love, and the whole disagreement begins when Balder wants to take Nanna for himself. In the Icelandic story, Hod is Balder's blind brother (Saxo does not have Hother as blind or as any relative of Balder) who inadvertently kills Balder with a mistletoe dart through the influence of Loki (Loki and mistletoe are not mentioned at all in Saxo's work).

In the Icelandic story, Balder is almost unkillable — the mistletoe is the only thing in the world that could kill him. The situation in Saxo's version is similar or analogous. It is said that Balder cannot be harmed by steel. But Hother goes on a long quest to get a certain sword, very hard and very sharp, and he does later give Balder a fatal wound, presumably with this same sword. Saxo does not give a name to this sword, but it is perhaps relevant that the dwarf (Saxo calls the creature a *satyr* of the woods) who Hother got the sword from is called Mimming.

There are also reflections of other legends in Saxo's version of this story.

Here, *Mimming* is the name of a dwarf who holds an unbeatable sword. In the *Didrik saga* (*Thidrekssaga*), *Mymming* is the name of an unbeatable sword. Here, Balder's skin is said to be so hard that steel cannot bite into it, but he is wounded and killed by Mimming's sword. In the *Didrik saga*, it is Sigurd the dragonslayer whose skin becomes so hard that steel cannot bite into it after he washes himself in dragon's blood. Sigurd does fear one sword though, and he refuses to fight against that sword. That is the sword Mymming.

Again, Saxo does not mention mistletoe at all in his account of the death of Balder. He is killed by a special sword. It is perhaps noteworthy, though, that *Mistilteinn* (meaning *mistletoe*) is found as the name of a sword in some other Old Norse sources (there are also other Norse sword names ending in *-teinn*).

Another interesting aspect of this legend is that it contains a rare example of Saxo writing about the god Thor. There are a couple of things in Saxo's description of Thor fighting in the battle that deserve comment. First, he has a club (Latin: *clava*) rather than a hammer as is typical in Icelandic writings and other surviving Scandinavian artworks. Perhaps this difference in words is more due to translation and language issues rather than any real difference in tradition. The second point though, is to do with the short handle of Thor's weapon. Saxo writes that the club is rendered useless when Hother cuts off its handle. In Icelandic accounts, a short handle is also an important part of the story of Thor's hammer. But there the hammer is actually made with a short handle. The short handle is meant to be a flaw, limiting the abilities of the hammer, and caused by Loki's interfering with the dwarfs who are making it. But the hammer nevertheless becomes famed and feared as a weapon despite this flaw. Much later in the *Gesta Danorum* (Book XIII), Saxo mentions that certain hammers were used by worshippers of Thor (there Saxo calls him *Jove*, the name of the Roman thunder god) in some of their ceremonies, and there he uses the Latin word *malleus* (meaning *hammer*).

Saxo also includes some classic viking imagery in his text. There is a description of a shield wall, and also a funeral pyre on a boat.

* * *

The idea of *Balder's dreams* echoes the Icelandic stories. But in Saxo's account there are two quite different ideas of what Balder's dreams might be. In a first series of dreams, he is tormented by Nanna, who he cannot have as she has married Hother. In the second, he is troubled by the image of a goddess of the underworld calling him to her, thus signalling his impending death. Note that in my rendition of the story I have called this goddess *Hel* — Hel is a Norse goddess associated with the underworld who does appear in Icelandic versions of this story. But Saxo calls her *Proserpina* (Persephone), the name of a Roman goddess also associated with the underworld. This second series of dreams is reminiscent of a scene from the poem *Balder's Dreams* (from the *Poetic Edda*), where a seeress tells Odin about how she sees in a vision the goddess Hel making preparations for Balder's arrival in the underworld (that poem doesn't actually say what Balder's bad dreams are about).

In this legend, Saxo also introduces the idea of Balder's being associated with a spring or a stream: he describes two quite different scenarios where Balder causes streams to start running. First, Balder brings forth a spring from the earth to reward his soldiers after a victory in battle. Second, a spring bursts from his burial mound to deter grave robbers. Perhaps this could, as has been suggested, be a way of explaining a local place name. Perhaps it could be wordplay. Perhaps it could represent an association of Balder with springs that is not known from surviving Icelandic sources. The idea of springs being formed after significant events is not uncommon in folklore and legend. The fact that Saxo mentions this idea twice in association with Balder surely lends it some significance.

A third idea about Balder that appears twice in Saxo's account is the idea that he cannot walk: just before the second battle against Hother (when Balder defeats Hother for the first time), we hear that Balder cannot walk because he is so ill and has to travel everywhere by carriage. And just before Balder's last battle, we hear that he has been wounded so badly by Hother that he cannot walk, and has to be carried into battle. Again, this repetition may perhaps echo some characteristic associated with Balder.

* * *

Supernatural wood maidens appear at several points in this story, apparently hoping to help both Hother and Balder in their ongoing battle against each other. As usual, we are left wondering what these wood maidens might have been called in the original Old Norse before Saxo translated them into Latin. Perhaps they correspond to *disir*. At any rate, they seem to be female guardian spirits with the power to influence the outcome of battles and other events.

* * *

The part of the story that deals with Odin's revenge is similar and consistent with what is known from the Icelandic stories. Rinda is mentioned in Icelandic sources (as *Rind*). In Snorri's *Prose Edda*, it is written that she is the mother of Vali (the avenger of Balder), and that she is "counted as a goddess". It is also written in *Sigurdardrapa* that Odin used magic (*seidr*) on her. This type of magic was associated with women, and its use by men was considered to be very shameful. Beyond this though, Icelandic sources are sparse on the detail.

So Saxo's detailed treatment gives a version of this story that is missing from Icelandic sources. Saxo's story also has Odin using magic on Rinda and also disguising himself as a woman before raping her, which then led to his disgrace and exile from his position as leader of the gods. (Of course, Saxo also gives a second account of Odin's exile.)

We know in general from Icelandic sources that Odin often calls himself by many different names. In Saxo's story, we are told two of the names Odin uses for himself while he is in disguise. They are *Roster* (while he is a smith), and *Wecha* (while he is a healing woman). The name *Roster* (maybe a corruption of *Rofter*) is also seen in Icelandic sources as *Hropt*, one of the many alternative names of Odin.

* * *

4, 6. ODIN's DISGRACE and EXILE (1; from Book III); and ODIN's DISGRACE and EXILE (2; from Book I)

Saxo includes two accounts of Odin's exile (Chapters 4 and 6). Although the reasons for the exile are quite different, the exile itself is described in a similar way.

In both accounts, when Odin is banished another god is chosen to become the leader of the gods. In the story from Book I, we are not told who this god is, only that he calls himself *Mith-Odin* while he is in charge. In the version from Book III, we are told that it is Oller (the Icelandic Ullr) who becomes the new leader, and that he takes Odin's name as well as his position as leader.

In both cases, Odin returns after a while to rule the gods again. In the version from Book I, this is due to the death of Frigg, whose quarrel with Odin resulted in his exile. In the version from Book III, Odin's redemption comes simply from the passage of time, or alternatively from his buying his way back in after some time had passed.

In both cases, the god who had taken charge was then driven into exile himself (to Sweden or Finland), and was soon killed.

* * *

These two episodes give a rare glimpse in Saxo's writing of some of the other Norse gods. Oller (Ullr) appears in Book III (Chapter 4). He is hardly described in detail, but Saxo does mention that he has a magical way of travelling over water. Saxo says the same thing about Odd (Frode's kinsman, and apparently a representation of a god as he can also control the weather; see Chapter 11). We read that Oller is able to travel over water by using a bone carved with runes, but it is not clear how this magic worked in practice.

When it comes to the Norse gods, Ullr is a curious case. He has a big name (meaning *glory*), and several places in Scandinavia seem to be named after him. And yet relatively little is known about him from Icelandic sources. We know from Snorri's *Prose Edda* that he is known for his good skiing and shooting (see also the notes to Chapter 22). Snorri also writes that *Ullr's ship* is a kenning for a shield. It is not obvious why this should be — the magical way of travelling across water (without a ship) that Saxo mentions may be related, but again it is not obvious how.

Odin's wife Frigg plays a major role in the story from Book I (Chapter 6). Her unfaithfulness to her husband is also mentioned in *Lokasenna* in the *Poetic Edda*. There, she sleeps with Odin's brothers, but in Saxo's story it is with a servant.

* * *

5. The GODS and the GIANTS (from Book I)

This is Saxo's explanation of some of the supernatural creatures of the Norse world. But as he is writing in Latin, it is impossible to know with any certainty the original Norse names of the beings he is describing here. And it is not always easy to draw parallels between what Saxo says here about his three classes of beings with what we read from Icelandic materials.

It seems likely that the giants (*gigantes*) are the *jotnar*, usually called giants in English. Saxo makes much of the giants' enormous size, which shows that at the time he was writing, this was understood to be a key characteristic of these creatures.

The two groups of gods Saxo describes are rather less obvious. He doesn't name either of the groups, nor does he say which gods belong to which, nor does he even call either of them gods — he calls them magicians, which is one of Saxo's main ways of referring to the gods. Snorri also describes two groups of gods — the *aesir* and *vanir* — but it is difficult to map what we know of these groups onto Saxo's description. The idea that one or other of these two groups of gods is the result of coupling between giants and the other group of gods doesn't seem to be consistent with what we might read from Icelandic sources. There is hardly enough information given in the brief description to get a good idea of how Saxo understood these groups of the old gods.

* * *

7–8. THORKILL's JOURNEY to VISIT GEIRROD; and THORKILL's JOURNEY to UTGARD (from Book VIII)

The stories of Thorkill's visits to Geirrod (*Geruthus*) and to Utgardaloki (*Utgarthilocus*) show a different side of Saxo's approach to storytelling. It is clear that these two episodes are related to the two stories of Thor's journeys to the land of the giants to visit Geirrod and Utgardaloki in the Icelandic tradition. It is also clear from Saxo's descriptions that in both of his journeys, Thorkill leaves his usual world — the world of men — behind, and travels to some hideous otherworld or underworld.

There is an obvious similarity in the names of the main protagonists: as well as the two giants having clearly similar names, Thorkill has a name similar to Thor. It is perhaps worth mentioning that in Swedish and Norwegian versions of the medieval ballad *Hammarhämtningen* (which tells the unmistakable story of Thor's journey to retrieve his stolen hammer from the troll Thrym, corresponding to *Thrymskvida*), Thor's name is given as *Thorkal*, *Thorekar*, *Thorkarl*, etc.

And yet we can be sure that Thorkill is not simply a euhemerised version of Thor in alternative versions of these legends — at least not all the time. Because when Thorkill is in Geirrod's chamber, the sight he sees is the aftermath of Thor's visit. Geirrod lies slumped and wounded from the iron bar that Thor has thrown through his body. The half-dead giantesses correspond to Geirrod's daughters Greip and Gjalp, whose backs were broken when, in the Icelandic story, Thor landed on them in his chair. Through Thorkill's words to the men, Saxo even tells us a very brief summary of what happened in the more familiar Thor myth.

And so it seems that in these stories, Saxo is making Thorkill a kind of human reflection of the god Thor. And Thorkill's journeys retrace and echo Thor's journeys in a way that is not the same as simple euhemerisation. Saxo is using Thorkill to explore the myths without becoming too directly involved.

Having said that, the supernatural is definitely very much present in these stories, and Thorkill's journeys to the other/underworld are filled with detailed descriptions of how he makes the journey, and of the generally rather unpleasant landscapes he finds when he arrives there.

Saxo's Utgardaloki is rather unlike the Utgardaloki who appears in Icelandic legend. It is possible that Saxo's bound god/giant is actually Loki, bound in chains while snakes fly overhead spitting poison. *Utgard* refers simply to the *place outside*, the *other place*, or the *otherworld*.

Another giant who appears in the first of the Thorkill legends is Gudmund. Gudmund is called Geirrod's brother, and he lives on the edge of the river that separates the world of men from the world of monsters, and he acts as a ferryman for Thorkill and his men when they want to cross over. But Gudmund also tries to get Thorkill and his men to stay with him for ever: he offers them various tempting gifts, and if they accept they would lose their minds and never be able to leave. Gudmund is unusual in that he seems to live in quite a nice place — the other giants visited by Thorkill all live in fairly hideous surroundings.

This Gudmund is also known from various Icelandic sagas, where he rules over a land called *Glæsisvellir* (*the glittering plain*) in Jotunheim. This is a land of eternal youth, which seems to correspond closely to Saxo's account.

The idea of visiting a supernatural creature (in the mountains, but also sometimes under the sea) and being given a drink of forgetfulness that causes our protagonist to forget their former life and fall in love with the one offering the drink, is common in the medieval Scandinavian ballads. *Den Bergtagna* is a classic example of this, but there are several others. This seems to be exactly the same idea as Gudmund's food and drink and other gifts.

* * *

There are some details in these stories that are curiously reminiscent of aspects of Norse mythology from Icelandic sources. Two of the objects held in Geirrod's hall are notable for their possible link to Frey's weapons: Frey had a sword that could fight by itself, and when he lost that sword he had to fight using a stag's antler.

In another interesting detail, the roof of Geirrod's hall is said to be made of spears. This architectural feature is more usually associated with Valhalla in Icelandic sources.

* * *

9. SYRITHA and OTTAR (from Book VII)

There has been speculation that this story is derived from an otherwise lost Freyja myth, and that Syritha is Freyja herself. It could be a rendition of the love story of Freyja and Od, not found in surviving Icelandic tradition, but referred to in passing. There is a similarity in names: Saxo's *Otharus* could be a Latinisation of the name *Od*. Neither is it too far-fetched that Freyja should be called Syritha, as she has a similar name, *Syr* (meaning *sow*), in some Icelandic texts (*Gylfaginning, Skaldskaparmal, Nafnathulur*), and Syritha could be a Latinisation of that name.

Alternatively, in the Icelandic stories, apart from Freyja's missing husband Od, we may also hear about her connection with a certain character called Ottar, who she transforms into a boar when they go to visit a seeress. This seeress accuses Freyja of being the lover of this boar, Ottar, which would strengthen the already strong, though obscure, connection to the sow. The connection between the name *Ottar* with the Latin *Otharus* is also very clear.

But there seems to be little in Saxo's story beyond this similarity of names to suggest a connection with Freyja. Syritha's character, keen to hide herself away, does not remind us of what we know of Freyja. Syritha's story is not dissimilar to that of Alfhild (Chapter 27), and we are told that Alfhild had a remarkable and complete change of character when she went from being a very modest girl to a viking woman warrior overnight.

Many of the notes in the 1905 translation of Saxo's work are based on Rydberg's overenthusiastic interpretations. It seems likely though that some more conservative conclusions have some truth in them, and that Freyja could be linked to Syritha just as Frey is linked to Frode (see below).

* * *

Saxo offers two ways that the giant may have abducted Syritha. In my retelling of the story, I have gone with the idea that the giant dressed as a woman to enter Syritha's household and gain her confidence. Saxo says that some people tell the story differently: that the giant persuaded a treacherous woman to enter Syritha's household and bring the girl out walking to a place where the giant could seize her.

This story has echoes in several medieval Scandinavian ballads. The account of how a man disguises himself as a woman to enter a maiden's house before inviting her out walking and then abducting her is found in *Valivan*. The account of a young man going away to the mountains to search for his girlfriend who has been abducted by a troll is found in *Heming and the Mountain Troll* (*Heming och Bergatrollet*). And a story where a girl is invited to a wedding between her lover and another woman, and then told to carry a torch to light the way to the bridal bed is told in *Lord Peter and Little Kerstin* (*Herr Peder och Liten Kerstin*).

* * *

10, 12, 13. FRODE's BRIDAL QUEST for HANUNDE; FRODE's BRIDAL QUEST for ALFHILD; and FRODE's PEACE and the END of FRODE (from Book V)

Saxo spends a lot of time on Frode, and there are some aspects of his story that link him with the god Frey. Frode is associated with a great peace that happened on Earth when Christ was born. Snorri also writes the same thing about a king called Frodi, and says that this Frodi ruled in Denmark at the same time that Frey ruled in Sweden.

The curious story about Frode's death (or what happens after his death) is also linked to Frey. Saxo tells how Frode's noblemen preserved his body and carried it around the country in a carriage for three years to give the illusion that he was still alive, and so prolong the peace that he had created. Snorri tells something similar about Frey: that his death was deliberately concealed for three years to prolong a period of peace and prosperity. Another Icelandic source tells how an idol of Frey was moved around in a carriage. Furthermore, there is also Tacitus's 1st century account of the Germanic goddess Nerthus, also associated with peace and fertility, also involved in ceremonies with human sacrifice (compare below where I mention Saxo's descriptions of ceremonies and human sacrifices to honour the god Frey), and who was also carried around in a carriage.

We may wonder how much more of Saxo's Frode is based on Frey, and consider the two stories of how brides are fetched for Frode. Similarities with the Icelandic story told in *Skirnismål*, about how Skirnir travels to the underworld to bring back the giantess Gerd to marry Frey, have been noticed in the past. Considering the case of Hanunde, the similarities are more or less these: Frode (or Frey) stays at home while messenger(s) are sent to a faraway land; the girl is unimpressed at first, and has no intention of marrying Frode (or Frey); she is persuaded by arguments and drugs; she marries Frode (or Frey).

After Erik kills Frode's foster family and becomes his new advisor, Erik then undertakes a similar mission on Frode's behalf to get him a second wife, Alfhild. It is perhaps notable how the foster family (portrayed as the baddies) win the girl using tactics not unlike Erik's (the goody). Both Grep and his mother Gotwara are said to be skilled speakers (just as Erik is). And Gotwara drugs Hanunde to make her more susceptible to their arguments, just as Erik's stepmother Kraka later drugs Alfhild. But really, the link between these two stories and the Norse myth of Frey, Gerd, and Skirnir seems rather tentative.

If we were to look in the world of the medieval Scandinavian ballads, we might find a story with a possibly more likely link to the Frey, Gerd, Skirnir myth in the ballad *Stallbröderna / The Stablemates*. I am not sure that the parallels between *Stallbröderna* and *Skirnismål* have been recognised before, although there are links between other poems of the *Poetic Edda* and medieval ballads: *Thrymskvida* and *Hammarhämtningen*; and *Svipdagsmål* and *Ungen Svejdal*. It may be that this ballad could also give a clue about the identity of the enigmatic Skirnir.

The ballad plot is summarised briefly as follows: there are two (usually unnamed) stablemates, I will call them here stablemates I and II; stablemate I offers stablemate II a horse if he helps him to find a bride; they ride away (they go together, but stablemate II takes the lead in everything, while stablemate I complains often that he wants to go home); they pass many terrible things, perhaps suggestive of entering an otherworld — these might include a bloody river, a wolf eating a man's leg, a forest of dead trees, a fence topped with dead men's heads; they meet and pass a gatekeeper who is reluctant to let them enter the girl's house; they find the girl they have come for, and she resists their advances; she is suddenly persuaded to change her mind, and she marries stablemate I.

The medieval ballads usually each have many variant texts, and when I translated *The Stablemates* for *Warrior Lore*, I used a variant where the stablemates were able to get the girl to change her mind using persuasive arguments. But in several variants of this ballad there is a twist during the argument with the girl: stablemate II reveals himself to be the girl's brother. "Stop fighting us, sister," he says. "This man I have brought is a good match for you."

It is certainly worth considering whether or not in the older myth told in *Skirnismål* there is also anything that suggests that Skirnir might be Gerd's brother. And there are indeed hints. When Gerd says: *"I fear the man standing outside killed my brother."* We may ask: *Who is Gerd's brother?* and *Who is Skirnir?* and indeed *What would it mean to the giants if one of them was to turn to the other side, and live with and serve the gods?* When Gerd asks him: *"Are you an elf, or are you one of the aesir or vanir?"* He replies no, he is none of those things. But Gerd does not ask him whether he is a giant like her.

If this poem was indeed acted out on stage, as has been suggested before, we may imagine that an enthusiastic audience already familiar with the story could be crying out at the players: *You killed my brother. I am your brother!*

Taking this back to Saxo, if it is an important part of the story that the messengers are actually related (brother/sister or otherwise) to the girl, then this seems to be absent in both of Saxo's Frode stories. It is certainly not mentioned explicitly, and a brother/sister relationship would seem to be impossible for both bridal missions. Having said that, it is Erik who suggests his kinswoman (fellow Norwegian) Alfhild as a likely candidate. And it is Westmar and Koll who suggest Hanunde the Hun.

* * *

Saxo does refer to the god Frey explicitly a few times in the *Gesta Danorum* text (he calls him *Fro*). In Book I, he tells how Hadding began a tradition of sacrifice to the god Frey: In Sweden, it was called *Froblot* (*Frey's blood feast*), and it was held there every year with the sacrifice of dark victims.

In Book III again, Saxo tells of human sacrifices to Frey taking place at Uppsala. In Book VI, Saxo gives a further description of the sacrifices to Frey at Uppsala: with players on stage, clapping and making effeminate gestures, and ringing bells in an unmanly way. In Book VIII, many brave Swedish warriors are described as kinsmen of the god Frey. Of course, these are mainly descriptions of worship practices rather than any myths about the god himself.

Saxo also names the King of Sweden defeated by Ragnar Lodbrok and Ladgerda in Norway as *Fro* (the same name he uses for Frey; see Chapter 28).

* * *

11. ERIK and FRODE (from Book V)

This legend introduces Erik the well-spoken, who goes on to become Frode's right-hand man. It is not clear who the inspiration for this Erik was, and probably Saxo based him on a source that is now lost. Part of how Erik earns his nickname is through constantly speaking wise sayings in the form of proverbs. Some of these proverbs are known from Icelandic sources as well as through Saxo's Latin translations.

Erik's father is called the "great hero" Ragnar, and his stepmother is Kraka. Kraka clearly has magical powers, and Saxo tells us that she is close to the gods. It seems that these two figures are very like Ragnar Lodbrok and Aslaug (whose nickname was *Kraka*), even though they fall well outside the timeline allotted to Ragnar Lodbrok by Saxo, and separate from the rest of his mentions in the *Gesta Danorum*.

The character of Odd also seems to be godlike. He can control the weather, and is said to be a friend to farmers as well as being feared by seafarers. He also has the curious magical power of being able to travel over water without a boat. Saxo also gives this ability to the god Oller (Chapter 4).

The names of Frode's foster family, *Westmar*, *Koll*, and *Gotwara* do not seem to be known in Icelandic sources. The name *Grep*, shared by three of Westmar's sons, is reminiscent of the giants' name, *Greip*. In Norse myth, *Greip* is the name of a giantess, one of the daughters of Geirrod, so unrelated to the three Greps featured in this story. But *Grep* may also be a generic name for giants (see notes on Chapter 24). It is not clear why there are three Grep triplets in the Erik story. Grep is named as an opponent who Erik defeats or humiliates more than once, but the killing of any of the Greps (mentioned by name) is only described once (all the other brothers were killed out on the ice).

* * *

It is worth commenting on the riddle episode when Erik gives Frode an explanation of what he did on his journey, and Frode doesn't understand a word of it. Erik explains the meaning of the last part of the riddle to Frode: when he said *Odd*, he meant the point of a spear, and so he was saying that he had killed the king's kinsman Odd — this is a fairly obvious pun for Old Norse speakers as the meaning of the name *Odd* is *point*, as in spear point. The rest of the riddle is left for us to speculate on.

I believe that the whole riddle is a long description of how Eric defeated Odd. First, when Saxo tells the story of how Erik beat Odd, much is made of the great number of stones that Odd filled his ships with. So it makes sense that Erik should list many stones as part of his riddle. But however many stones Odd had brought with him, there was more sand in that place as they were at sea.

Second, the dolphins — we can speculate here. In Old Norse, the word for dolphin (*hnisa*) has been used to describe part of a ship. This word is used as an alternative to *husasnotra* in Orvar Odd's Saga to mean a wooden decorative part of a ship, probably the figurehead, often an animal's head. So it seems that in the riddle, Erik is listing the pieces of wrecked ships: the figureheads (dolphins), the masts (logs), the planks. Many trees were felled to make the boats that he destroyed, and yet there are many more trees than that in the woods. Alternatively, it may be that the fallen trees refer to the dead men — trees are used as a kenning for men in Norse poetry.

And then finally he explains how he killed Odd when he talks about the points of spears. So Saxo's description of Odd's defeat by Erik matches the riddle quite well.

* * *

14–17. HADDING and HARDGREP; HADDING and RAGNHILD, and HADDING's JOURNEY to the UNDERWORLD; HADDING's DAUGHTER; and The DEATHS of HUNDING and HADDING (from Book I)

Hadding is an interesting character in Saxo's work. He has several encounters with Odin. He travels to the underworld (more than once). And there is a very clear correlation between the story of Hadding and Ragnhild here and the story of Njord and Skadi from Icelandic sources.

There are two episodes involving the marriage of Hadding and Ragnhild that must be compared with corresponding episodes involving the marriage of Njord and Skadi. In the Icelandic sources, we may read that Skadi was invited to choose a husband from a line-up of gods where she could only see their ankles. She chose the one who she thought had the nicest ankles, expecting it to be Balder, and was disappointed when she found that she had picked Njord. In Saxo's legend, Ragnhild has to choose a husband from a line-up of suitors, and she does it by examining only their legs. But she is not aiming to choose the one with the nicest legs. She is looking for a token (a ring) that she had hidden earlier inside one of their legs.

When Njord and Skadi are married, they disagree about where to live. Njord wants to live by the sea and Skadi in the mountains. Their differences of opinion about this are spoken in verse form. Similarly, Hadding does not enjoy peaceful life in the countryside with his wife, and he longs to return to viking life at sea. But Ragnhild greatly prefers inland life. Saxo includes a Latin translation of the Old Norse poem, now spoken by Hadding and Ragnhild. It is quite unmistakable, and is possibly the most recognisable passage of text in Saxo's work for anyone familiar with the surviving Icelandic sources. Nevertheless, Saxo's poem is rather longer than the Icelandic poem. Perhaps Saxo expanded on it himself, but as only a fragment of the Old Norse original survives, it is also possible that Saxo was translating further Old Norse stanzas that are now lost to us in the original language.

So it is clear that in part at least, Hadding seems to be associated with Njord. But there is plenty more to Hadding's story that does not seem to have a surviving parallel related to Njord in Icelandic sources.

* * *

Vagnhofdi and *Hafli* are given (together) in the list of the names of giants in Snorri's *Prose Edda*. *Hardgreip* is mentioned in the list of the names of giantesses. These names clearly correspond to Saxo's giants Wagnhofde, Hafle, and Hardgrep.

***

When Hadding visits the underworld with the woman, he sees several sights that are suggestive of the Old Norse beliefs. The everlasting battle where the warriors relive their final moments is reminiscent of Valhalla.

***

The old man who Hadding meets on the way to the battle in Bjarmeland is no doubt Odin. This is made clear when he teaches Hadding about the wedge fighting formation. This formation is usually called *svinfylking* in Old Norse as it resembles a pig's snout, and it is well known that it was used by Scandinavian warriors. See also Chapter 18 for another occasion when Odin teaches one of his favoured warriors about the wedge formation.

***

Saxo also has other stories about Hadding and his encounters with the gods that I have not told here, but that could be interesting for those who want to read further. After Hardgrep's death, he is befriended by an old man who has lost an eye (no doubt this is Odin). Saxo's description of everything that happens between them is tantalising, but unfortunately very brief. It involves: a magical restorative drink, a prophecy, a trip to the underworld on horseback across the sea, the gaining of superhuman strength through the killing and eating of a lion, and other things. Later on, Hadding has yet another encounter with the gods when he finds and kills an unknown animal. An old woman then appears who tells him that he has killed a god.

***

18. HARALD, ODIN, and the WEDGE FORMATION (from Books VII–VIII)

The battle between Ring and Harald is usually called the battle of Bråvellir, and it is also mentioned in various Icelandic sagas. The battle of Bråvellir is also the setting for the Swedish legend of Blenda, where an army of Swedish women defeated an army of invading Danes. Saxo does mention warrior women in his description of the battle, fighting alongside the men.

The name that Odin adopts in this story is *Brun*. And *Brun* (meaning *brown*, or maybe *bear*), appears in the list of Odin's names in Snorri's *Prose Edda*.

This is one of two occasions where Saxo explains how Odin was the originator of the wedge fighting formation commonly called *svinfylking* in Old Norse (see also Chapter 15). The two descriptions of the formation are slightly different.

* * *

19–20. FRIDLEIF and the DRAGON (from Book VI); and FRODE and the DRAGON (from Book II)

The stories of Fridleif and the dragon and of Frode and the dragon are almost exactly similar. These are some of the details that are the same: first our hero is given instructions on what to do (in a song or in a dream); the dragon lives on an island; the dragon is first seen by water; the dragon's back is resistant to attack; the dragon has poisonous spit; our hero protects himself from the poison using oxhide; the dragon is killed by attacking its belly; the dragon was guarding a great treasure, buried underground; our hero gets the treasure.

These two dragonslayer legends are similar to the legend of Sigurd, which is nowadays much better known. Saxo doesn't tell about any dragonslayers by that name, though.

Note that the way Saxo tells it, this Frode the dragonslayer is not the same as the Frode who was helped by Erik (Chapters 10–13), nor the Frode who fought Froger (Chapter 32).

* * *

21. AMLETH (from Book III)

The legend of Amleth is essentially familiar to many modern readers as it inspired Shakespeare's play, *Hamlet*. Shakespeare's storyline seems to be fairly loosely based on the legend as told by Saxo. But the main plotline is similar: Our hero's evil uncle murders the hero's father and marries his mother. Our hero pretends to be mad, and then avenges his father by killing the uncle.

When we look for anything resembling Amleth's story in Icelandic sources, there is not a lot to be found. In Snorri's *Prose Edda*, there is a tantalising mention of an *Amlodi* in a kenning-heavy verse relating to the sea, but it seems that this is all there is. This verse, by a poet called Snaebjorn, describes the sea as a mill, turned by the nine women (the waves). And it tells that the turning of this mill grinds flour (sand) from Amlodi's drink (the sea). This must surely be linked to Amleth's riddling remarks in Saxo's story: when Feng's men tell Amleth to look at the huge piles of flour and show him the sandhills by the seashore, he replies that they must have been milled by an enormous mill (the sea).

Amleth's father is called Horwandil, which seems also to be related to an Old Norse name, *Aurvandil*. *Aurvandil* may be the name of a star. He appears in Snorri's *Prose Edda* as the wife of the witch Groa, and his toe is flung into the heavens by Thor to become a star. This doesn't seem to be clearly related to the Amleth story, and little else about Aurvandil survives.

An essentially similar but much more abbreviated version of the Amleth legend is told in *Chronicon Lethrense* (also written in Denmark in Latin, slightly earlier than Saxo).

In Amleth's pretended madness and speaking in riddles, he tries to tell the truth while wanting at the same time to seem to be talking nonsense. Some of his double meanings work as well in modern English and modern Danish as they must have done in Old Norse. When Amleth is telling Feng's men where he had sex with the girl, he makes it sound ridiculous: on a colt's foot, on a cock's comb, and on a roof (or thatch, the same word in Danish). But these are all the names of marsh plants in Danish: *Tussilago*, *Rhinanthus*, and *Phragmites*. Two of these plants have the same common names in English (coltsfoot and cockscomb).

I changed one of Amleth's riddles in my telling of the story: about the rudder as an enormous knife. I wrote that it would cut deep (as an enormous knife would cut a big cut, but also the deep is the sea). Saxo had that it would be used to cut a similarly enormous ham (also referring to the sea, but presumably in a way that puns on an Old Norse word for ham).

* * *

Saxo does tell a further legend about Amleth that I have not included here (in Book IV). He tells how Amleth returns to Britain and marries a second wife, thanks in part to a wonderful shield he has covered in pictures of battles being fought and great deeds being done.

* * *

22. TOKE (from Book X)

This Toke also appears in the *Jomsvikinga saga* as Palnatoki. The story told here is in two parts, the first involving shooting and the second skiing, and very similar versions of both parts of the story have been told about other figures of myth and legend. Sometimes the stories only involve shooting, sometimes skiing and shooting, and sometimes even more sports.

The combination of excellence in archery and skiing points tantalisingly towards the god Ullr, who it seems was once so important, but about who so little survives. In Snorri's *Prose Edda*, it is written that Ullr is so good at skiing and archery that no-one can beat him.

There are several versions of the legend that closely resemble the shooting episode. From Scandinavia, there are the stories of Heming Aslaksson / Gauti Aslaksson in a Norwegian ballad, a Faeroese ballad, and an Icelandic *thattr*; and also the enigmatic mythological archer Egil in the *Didrik saga*. Possibly the most famous version of the legend, with William Tell, comes from Switzerland. And there is also a version of the story in an English ballad, where the archer is called William of Cloudsley.

Most of these stories have features in common. For example, in most of them, our hero takes out two arrows from his quiver, and after successfully making the first shot, explains to the king that the second arrow would have been for him if he had failed.

Egil is a mythological figure associated with archery. He appears as the brother of Weland the smith in the *Didrik saga* as well as in the *Poetic Edda*. The *Didrik saga* makes much of his archery skills. As well as the master-shot with the apple, he also hunts many birds so that Weland can use their feathers to make his bird suit. And he also makes a second master-shot to fool the king, pretending to shoot at Weland in flight, but in fact aiming for a bag of blood he is carrying. Egil also appears on the Anglo-Saxon Franks casket, where he is named in runes, and pictured apparently defending a building containing a woman using his bow and arrows. Any narrative description of this legend is lost. But bizarrely, the William of Cloudsley ballad mentioned above also features an episode where Cloudsley defends his wife and children from a mob surrounding their house using his bow and arrows.

The skiing episode is also an important part of the legend for some of those versions mentioned above. The three versions featuring Heming Aslaksson / Gauti Aslaksson (a Norwegian ballad, a Faeroese ballad, and an Icelandic *thattr*) all include a skiing trial with different outcomes in each case. It is perhaps also worth noting that the antagonist in all these three is a different King Harald: Harald Hardrada. In at least two of these versions of the legend there were further sporting trials, including a second archery challenge and a swimming competition (maybe involving wrestling in the water).

* * *

23. ALFHILD and ALF (from Book VII)

The first part of Alfhild's story shares features with the stories of Thora (Chapter 29), whose father brings her two snakes to look after, and also Syritha (Chapter 9), who refuses to look at any of the men who come to see her.

After she refuses to marry Alf (under her mother's influence), Alfhild has a major character change and becomes a viking warrior woman. Saxo names several other famous warrior women throughout his work, but he does not tell their stories in as much detail as Alfhild. They include Sela (Book III), Rusla (Book VIII), Wisna (Book VIII), and Vebjorg (Book VIII). The story of Ladgerda (Chapter 28) is also included in this book.

* * *

24. GRAM, GROA, and BESS (from Book I)

The names *Gram* and *Groa* are both known from other Norse legends, though there is no clear link to the characters in this story. Gram is the name of Sigurd's sword that was reforged. Groa is the name of Svipdag's mother, who he raised from the dead to help him on his quest. And Groa is also the name of a witch who was supposed to (but did not) pull a rock out of Thor's head that had got stuck in there.

In Saxo's text, Gram tells Groa that he has "come from Grip" (I don't mention this detail in my telling of the story). Here, *Grip* might be supposed to be the name of the giant she is engaged to marry. It may be that she supposes that the giant who Gram is pretending to be is Grip's brother. A similar name, *Grep*, is used for one of Erik's antagonists in Chapters 10 and 11, and the name is also reminiscent of the Norse giant(ess) name *Greip*.

* * *

25. FRIDLEIF and the ROBBERS (from Book VI)

The twelve robber brothers in this story all have names ending *-bjorn*, meaning *bear*. It seems that they are supposed to represent a group of twelve berserkers (bear warriors). It has been noted before that groups of twelve berserkers, sometimes with bear names, are mentioned in several Icelandic sagas. The fact that they live on an island and leave it only to spread fear and destruction throughout the surrounding area is reminiscent of the story of Angantyr the berserker and his eleven brothers as told in the *Saga of Hervor and Heidrek* (Saxo does include a version of the Angantyr story in Book VI). Another instance in Old Norse literature of a group of twelve berserkers being attacked on an island (a big one: Zealand) while they are asleep is found in *Hrolf Kraki's Saga* (Saxo would also be familiar with this as he includes a version of the story in Book II).

The Ofoot mentioned in this story as a giant and the former owner of Bjorn's dog could correspond to the Old Norse name *Ofoti*, which is the name of a giant. This Ofoti appears in *Orm Storolfssons Thattr*, where he is named as the father of the troll Bruse. There is nothing about a dog in the Old Norse text, but it does tell that Bruse's mother was an enormous black she-cat. (The story of Orm and Bruse and the troll cat is also told in medieval ballads including *Brusajøkils Kvad* from the Faeroes, and *Essbjorn Prude och Ormen Stark* and also *Ulf den Starke* from Sweden.) It may be that Ofoot's fierce dog is also supposed to be a bear.

∗ ∗ ∗

26. The EVERLASTING BATTLE: HAGEN, HEDIN, and HILDA (from Book V)

This legend is rather well known outside of Saxo's work. The battle is sometimes called *Hjadningavig*, and versions of the story appear in Snorri's *Prose Edda*, *Ragnarsdrapa*, *Sörla thattr*, and elsewhere. Often in these Old Norse versions it is not Hedin and Hagen (Hogni) themselves who Hild resurrects to continue fighting, but rather the many men who were killed in the great battle between the armies led by these two.

∗ ∗ ∗

27. HAGBARD and SIGNE (from Book VII)

The legend of Hagbard and Signe must have been relatively well known. It is alluded to in various Old Norse sources, including Snorri's *Ynglingasaga* and also the *Volsungasaga*. But Saxo's version of the story is far fuller and more complete than any surviving Old Norse source.

The story continued to be told for many centuries through a medieval ballad that was widespread and known in all the Scandinavian countries. The ballad, called *Habor och Signild* in Swedish, tells a story that is very close to Saxo's version, albeit in slightly abbreviated form, and starting from the moment that Hagbard disguises himself as a woman. By way of an introduction, the ballad also includes a dream Hagbard has, where he learns that he will die because of his love for a woman.

The ballad *Bendik and Årolilja*, probably best known in Norway, tells a rather similar story, especially in those variants of the ballad that have Bendik dressing up as a woman to gain access to Årolilja (not all variants of the ballad include this part).

* * *

The king's two advisors, Bilwis and Bolwis have names that recall a pair of Old Norse names. *Bileyg* and *Baleyg* are names for Odin according to *Grimnismål*, meaning *wavering-eye* and *flame-eye*. If these two names reflect the two very different eyes of the one-eyed god (one seeing and one blind), then it becomes relevant that Saxo states that one of the two advisors is blind. It has been suggested that the different approaches of the two advisors reflect the different sides of Odin's character.

A further pair of Old Norse names *Byleistr* (of obscure meaning) and *Helblindi* (meaning *all blind*) could be another similar pair to describe Odin's eyes. These names are given as Loki's brothers, but this would not necessarily be inconsistent with Loki's close relationship with Odin.

* * *

28–31. RAGNAR and LADGERDA; RAGNAR and THORA; RAGNAR and ESBJORN's DAUGHTER; and RAGNAR's DEATH (from Book IX)

There are several Old Norse sagas that tell stories about Ragnar, and Saxo has written a good deal about this figure. I have picked out only some of these stories: how he won two of his wives (Ladgerda and Thora), and also a third woman (Esbjorn's daughter), and how he died. Saxo does not mention Ragnar's third wife Kraka/Aslaug at all when he is writing about Ragnar in Book IX of *Gesta Danorum*, though he does name her sons. (A married couple called Ragnar and Kraka do appear elsewhere in *Gesta Danorum*, see the notes on Chapter 11.)

* * *

32. FRODE and FROGER (from Book IV)

Saxo tells us that Froger is a son of Odin, but little about this character seems to be known from elsewhere.

Saxo writes about several kings called Frode. Some of them seem to be related to Frey, but not all. The name *Frode* can mean both *wise* and *fruitful*, and much is made in this story of how Frode is able to defeat his opponent (who is favoured by the gods) using the power of his mind rather than brute force.

* * *

Bibliography

Translations

I have mainly used Oliver Elton's translation (with notes by Frederick York Powell), The First Nine Books of the Danish History of Saxo Grammaticus, Norroena Society, New York, 1905

Especially for the Toke skiing episode, I read the Danish translation by Frederik Winkel Horn, Saxo Grammaticus, Danmarks historie, 1896–1898

Other English translations:

Peter Fisher's translation, edited with commentary by Hilda Ellis Davidson Saxo Grammaticus: The History of the Danes, Books I-IX, Boydell and Brewer, 1979

Peter Fisher's translation, edited with commentary by Karsten Friis-Jensen Saxo Grammaticus: Gesta Danorum, The History of the Danes, Oxford University Press, 2015

General references

Hilda Ellis Davidson, Gods and Myths of Northern Europe, Penguin Books, 1964

John Lindow, Norse Mythology: A Guide to the Gods, Heroes, Rituals, and Beliefs, Oxford University Press, 2002

Specific references

Review on Skirnismål as a stage drama:
Rick McGregor, Skirnismål as Ritual Drama: A Summary of Scholarship this Century, Deep South, 1 (3), 1995

Dolphins (Erik's riddle):

> *hnisa*, in Richard Cleasby and Gudbrand Vigfusson, An Icelandic–English Dictionary, 1874; On *hnisa* and *husasnotra*: Orvar Odd's Saga in C. C. Rafn's edition of Fornaldar Sögur Nordrlanda, 1829, p. 210; On *husasnotra*: William Sayers, Karlsefni's husasnotra: The Divestment of Vinland, Scandinavian Studies, 75, 2003, 341–350.

Amleth's riddles:

> Hans Sperber, The Conundrums in Saxo's Hamlet Episode, PMLA, 64 (4), 1949, 864–870

Bears as "dogs of the gods":

> Frog, Volundr and the Bear in Norse Tradition, Selected Proceedings of the UCL Graduate Symposia in Old Norse Literature and Philology, 2008, 1–50.

For English translations of most of the Scandinavian ballads discussed here and references to sources, see books of ballad translations by Ian Cumpstey: Lord Peter and Little Kerstin; Warrior Lore; The Faraway North.